CW00540302

"A Nice Tailend From Mr Burrows"

Growing up in 1950s/1960s S6

By Jack Watson

Published by ACM Retro Ltd
Registered office :
51 Clarkegrove Road
Sheffield
S10 2NH

Visit ACM Retro at:
www.acmretro.com

Jack Watson asserts the moral right to be
identified as the author of this work.
A catalogue record for this book is available
from the British Library.

This work is dedicated to my wife
Christine,
the love of my life.
I thank her for putting up with my faults
and failures over these many years.
I also thank her for cooking regularly
the best stew and dumplings
in Christendom.

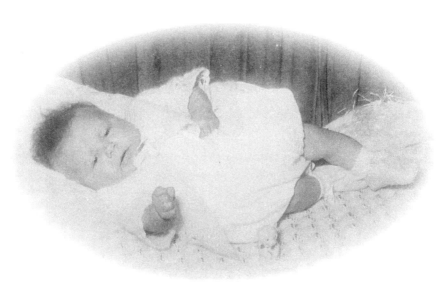

Jack - a big baby!

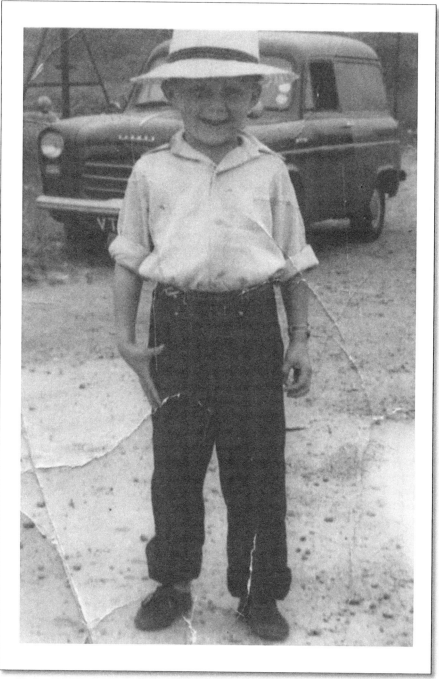

Jack in some back-end street in mid-fifties Sheffield

Contents

Preface

I had honestly never heard the term "baby boomer" until a few years ago. Now everyone says it. Well, maybe not everyone, but it is of course used in reference to the post-World War Two baby boom that occurred between 1946-1962.

On Wikipedia it points out that the "leading edge" baby boomers are those born between 1946-1955. Well bless my soul, I'm "leading edge".

It goes on to say that nowadays we boomers control over 80% of personal financial assets, and more than half of all consumer spending. This must surely only apply to western society. Also, and this is far more relevant to me, we buy 77% of all prescription drugs sold.

We are, it seems, enormously wealthy, deliriously happy, always satisfied, cuddly, lovable, cultured and surprisingly right wing (to such an extent that we almost verge on fascism). Well, that's not me, nor is it the generation I grew up with.

To be honest though, there is a tendency for people to vere right as they age. It's a natural progression. Idealism gives way to realism. Promiscuity gives way to monogamy. Testosterone gives way to a good meal. Opinions give way to "Oh, screw it."

Another thing is, and I may be wrong, but I don't think we had a wide circle of friends as such. Of course, we had strong acquaintances, but not a whole gaggle of mates. Well, I didn't anyway. Maybe we were encouraged to be individualistic, or maybe we held the opinion that nobody knows more than me, so why should I befriend them?

I never found the appeal in joining a group or club either. At the age of eight every lad I knew at school was joining the cubs as a forerunner to the boy scouts.

"Come on Jack , come to the Cubs, six o'clock on Friday". I shook my head in disapproval.

Coronation Street had just been born and it was like nothing I had ever seen before. (It's crap nowadays by the way). It was aired on Friday evenings in those days and I wouldn't have missed it for the world, let alone the Cubs.

I never felt the urge to be part of things. I didn't in later years feel the urge to be a mod, or a rocker, or a hippy, or a skinhead. I just sort of hovered between them all enjoying the music that each engendered. I was equally at home with The Who, Gene Vincent, Jefferson Airplane and Judge Dread.

Football was different of course. That gave you identity and comradery. However, I have decided to hardly mention the sport in this work because it is too heavily documented already, and it just bores the tits off most people, especially the type who have tits.

So, I will embark on this journey, and in the course of it will no doubt have my ailing memory jogged about happenings from over two generations ago. Please enjoy...

A young Jack, with his dad

Chapter 1
Somewhere (a place for us)

My first memory of anything, anywhere, ever, occurred on Proctor Place. It was late October 1954, and I was three years old. The sun was shining.

I had a small Union Jack flag on a stick for waving. Mrs Bullen, a neighbour, lifted me from the ground and held me tightly. Suddenly everyone was waving a flag. Hundreds of Union Jacks flashing a blur of red, white and blue.

"Wave Jackie, wave", she instructed. Suddenly several cars, the likes of which I had never seen before, began to pass us closely by.

"Wave at the Queen Jackie, wave."

I waved as hard as I could, and I'm sure Elizabeth the Second waved back at me that day. It was all rather like the opening scene of 'Born on the 4th of July', but without the firecrackers and limbless veterans.

Her majesty was on her way to Hillsborough football ground during her one day whistle stop tour of Sheffield.

The memory has lived with me all this time and I'm really quite proud to tell people the story of my first recollection of life here on Planet Earth.

I didn't know exactly how old I was when we came to live on Proctor Place but, I'm guessing I was about 18 months. Previously we had lived with my grandparents at 51 Balmain Road, Sutton Estate, and then for around six months at Birley Moor Way in South Sheffield. However, six months was enough there as my father wanted to be back in S6 because he missed it, and it was much nearer his work.

I'm so glad they made that decision. I swear I would not be anything like the person I am today if I had not lived at Proctor Place. As a child living there I didn't need a theme park, or a fun fair, or a puppet show. Everything I wanted was there at my command.

The house itself was falling apart. I think we rented it for about eight shillings a week. A Victorian building, sharing a yard with two other houses, it had so many faults and weaknesses it should probably have been condemned after World War Two.

The landlord was Mr. Swift, a man in his sixties I would guess, who owned all three houses and the row of shops just over the wall. If we had been on the Monopoly board, we would probably have been valued at £10.

We lived at number 4. At number 2 lived the widow Mrs Lee. At number 6 lived Mr Swift's son, Henry, along with his wife, Doreen, and children Philip and Shirley. Doreen's mother was Mrs Lee from number 2. It was all very close knit.

Each house had it's own outside toilet, which to be honest was a bit of a privilege as many back to back houses shared a toilet between two or three dwellings. Still, at least that way you could read other peoples' newspapers from the day before, or even the weekend.

The houses didn't have bathrooms or running hot water. All water had to be boiled up from cold. There was one coal fire in the back room downstairs. All the other rooms were cold and damp and unheated.

We had two rooms downstairs. The back room housed the sink, fireplace, television, radio, table and other stuff and was the room we occupied all the time. The front room was hardly ever used and we had in there a really nice sofa and chair, a radiogram and a fish tank. The only person who ever used that room was me, and that was just to listen to the racing results, cricket scores and Mrs Dale's Diary. Yes!

Upstairs were two bedrooms and an attic. I had one bedroom and my mum, dad and brother Alan (born 1960) had the other.

So we weren't too pushed for space. The house and outside area were decrepit though. The shared yard, which was used for drying washing and

Proctor Place (courtesy of Harry Ainscough and www.copperbeechstudios.co.uk)

as a playground for we kids, had been without surfacing for years. Several miniature sinkholes about 4 feet in diameter in the yard made it treacherous for anyone using it. Next door to the three houses was the place I loved from the first time I ever entered its doors. The Kinema.

The Kinema, a fabulous early 20th century cinema, originally opened its doors in November 1912 and, after alterations in 1920, had a seating

The Watson clan in 1957

capacity of 1202. During the Sheffield Blitz of December 1940 a land mine exploded causing severe damage. It re-opened in October 1941 and survived until July 1966. It was demolished shortly after.

As a lad I remember queues for the place stretching along Proctor Place and in to Middlewood Road. I often wonder how many people it sold entrance fees to during its 54 years of life. How many people fell in love there? How many people felt labour pains in there? How many tears of joy were shed in there? It had a magical atmosphere and it bred in me my love of heroes, adventure, gallantry, bravado and 'derring-do'. I didn't care how old the film was or who it starred, I was transfixed from the moment I sat down in there until the moment I came out.

During that period of the fifties and early sixties, the lights from the foyer of the Kinema illuminated Proctor Place during cold, dark winter nights. This provided us with a feeling of great inner warmth and comfort. Oh, happy days. I am so grateful for the Kinema's influence on my life.

We also had a chapel on the street. In fact it is still there. The Hillsborough Tabernacle Congregational Church. Our next door neighbours, the Swifts, were regulars there and were often involved in functions, garden parties etc organised by the church. As with the Kinema, the "tabs," as it was known, was damaged by the same land mine in the blitz. In fact not just damaged, but totally destroyed.

Bit by bit, from 1942 until May 1955, the church was rebuilt. I have a memory of helping glaziers put the final touches on windows in the building. They let me play with the putty and lift all sorts of tools and equipment for them. I could have been no more than three-and-a-half, and yet every time I smell putty now, I'm instantly taken back to spring 1955 along with all its wonderful sights and sounds.

Thinking back, me and my friend Lesley (female) used to wander all over from the age of three. We used to walk in shops and ask for biscuits, buns, sweets and ice creams. No money was exchanged. We didn't have any. Besides it always appeared somewhat unsightly to store a half crown piece inside a pair of tight fitting gold satin swimming trunks.

We went missing on one occasion and were found in the outside toilets of the Blue Ball pub on Bradfield Road. Can you imagine parents nowadays allowing kids as young as three to wander the streets unaccompanied for hours on end?

I loved Lesley and I will say even now that she was my very best friend ever. She was the second of four daughters and was somewhat different to her siblings in that she giggled continuously and joined in all the boys' games. She was great fun, and we laughed our way through childhood together. I still miss her.

Proctor Place is L-shaped and nowadays has no houses. At the time I am writing about, there were eight houses, a shop with the Bingley family living in the back and upstairs, a cinema, four shops including Bingley's flower shop, a bakery, a bolt and nut stockist, a furniture maker and of course a church. I knew each building inside out as I explored them - if not by daylight then at night. The Don Bakery gave off some terrific smells. Lesley and me would often just stroll into the bakery semi-naked as usual, and the workers would give us a doughnut or an egg custard perhaps. The bakery van drivers were complete nutters though and would never use their brakes until the very last second. As brave and streetwise as we were, we would always scatter when they took to the road.

The Bingley family not only used their building as a business, they also used it for accommodation. Their business was in flowers, fruit and vegetables. They sold flowers from the shop but also had a barrow to sell their wares on Roselle Street, just 30 yards away. Their son and daughter, Micheal and Vicky, were friends of mine and to this day they continue to run their business from a stall in Hillsborough precinct. They are both well in to their sixties.

Other kids on the street were Philip and Shirley Swift, both older than me. Shirley recently told me that Philip was a successful boat builder in the Lake District. He was, as I recall, always good with model aeroplanes and balsa wood as a kid. The Swifts left the street in November 1959 and moved to a nice semi-detached house on Garry Road, half a mile away. When they first moved they used to invite me to visit them to play 'New Footy' with Philip. 'New Footy' morphed later in to 'Subbuteo'.

Then there was the Whomersley family with sons, Roy and Alan. Roy was

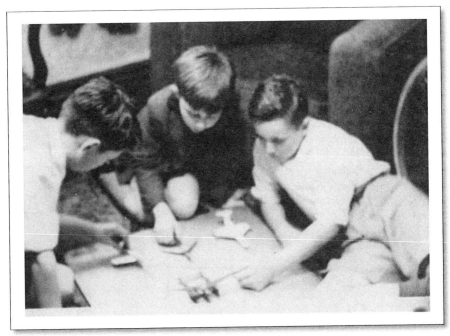

Jack with friends Roy Whomersley and Philip Swift

the same age as Philip Swift, and they were big buddies. I used to play football and cricket with them and generally follow them around everywhere. Alan Whomersley was a good seven or eight years older than me and played in goal for Sheffield boys when he was about 15.

The Swifts and the Whomersleys were nice, pleasant people and both families got on well together. One difference however. The Swifts supported Sheffield United, and the Whomersleys supported Sheffield Wednesday. In fact the Swifts were the only Blades I ever met until I went to King Edward VII at 12 years of age. S6 was solid Wednesday.

All the kids on Proctor Place attended Malin Bridge junior and infant school. That is apart from the Bingleys who were Roman Catholic, and went to Sacred Heart. None of us should have actually gone to Malin Bridge. We should have all attended Hillsborough junior and infants. Proctor Place is situated on the right-hand side of Middlewood Road. Strictly speaking we resided in Owlerton electoral ward, and all Owlerton kids went to Hillsborough school.

My father and mother were all for taking me to Hillsborough school, but I kicked up a fuss.

"I'm not going there."

13

"Yes you are. It will be good."

"I want to go to Malin Bridge. Philip and Roy go there."

"It's nearer for you to go to Hillsborough school."

"No, I'm not going."

"Well, we'll see."

See we did! Early September 1956 and my mother was dragging my weedy, skinny, reluctant body up the hills that lead to Malin Bridge School. I had won, yeeeesss. Or had I? I just didn't want to go through that door of the school and leave my mother for hours. Even though the teachers were encouraging me and generally being nice to me, I just didn't want to be there.

It took me two years to get over it. Every morning I would kick, punch and spit my way through the schoolyard bruising my mother, other kids' mothers, other kids, teachers, caretakers, and an assortment of parents' dogs just there for the walk.

The irony of it all was that I was good at schoolwork. In the end of term tests we took, I always finished with about 98% in English, arithmetic and telling the time. Only the imperious Stephen Nicholson bettered me.

In more recent years I have come to realise that the decision I made before I was five-years-old to go to Malin Bridge School was probably the biggest single decision I ever made in my life. My girlfriend, wife and mother of my children, Christine, just three months younger than me, went to Hillsborough school. If I had been press ganged in to attending the same school, I would have been in the same classroom as her for the next six or seven years. I am sure we might have been good friends with each other, but to go on to marry? I very much doubt it.

So, in hindsight, because I followed Philip and Roy around like a lapdog, and wanted to be in the same school, it led me to go and meet the woman I would marry years later.

"Sometimes you meet someone, and before you know their name, before you know where they are from, you know that some time in the future, this person is going to mean something to you." That perfect quotation may never have applied.

Proctor Place was my place. Despite its urban decay and its full on way of life (even in the relatively sedate fifties), it had a buzz unlike anywhere I have lived since. It is at the heart of the Hillsborough district, and as such it took me in, nurtured me, educated me, supported me, looked after me.

Sadly, on a very snowy late November day in 1965, the removal van arrived and shuffled the four of us away to the cold north west hills of our city, leaving behind the melting ice on the pavements I had played on for 12 years...

Chapter 2
Heroes & Villains (mid-fifties)

I have read that 11th April, 1954, was officially declared the most boring day of the 20th century as nothing significant happened, and there were no births or deaths of note. Well, excuse me, but I bet that all around the globe on that date women were pushing and bearing down in their numbers in an effort to give birth. It was pretty significant to them I reckon.

Then of course people were dying, all around the globe. I bet the poor sods weren't exactly sat up in bed saying "God I'm bored. I wish something significant would happen."

Well try ceasing to breathe, not just for three minutes like some South Seas pearl diver, but for ever and ever, amen. For perpetuity.

What is significant to one man is completely insignificant to the next man. In Alabama during 1954 a 4kg piece of meterorite crashed through the roof of a house and severely bruised a sleeping woman. It could have been much worse for her. Say for example she had lived on Bikini Atoll. In March of that year a massive H bomb was tested setting the sea, the sky, and the Marshall Islands on fire. Utter devastation. What if that woman from Alabama had been on holiday there on Bikini Atoll? Where would she have finished up? Johannesbourg?

Talking of Africa, when I was very small, say three-years-old, in the last quarter of 1954, I remember the news on our very basic black and white Murphy television set. The newscasters at that time were always mentioning the Mau Mau tribe of Kenya, and their rebellious antics . I honestly remember thinking they were called Mau Mau because they kept cats.

I would have loved to have had a much better recollection of 1954. It seemed very much a fun year. Good things happened. Marilyn Monroe married Joe Di Maggio, and although Marilyn moved on to other men during the remaining years of her life, Joe forever loved her until his dying day.

Roger Bannister ran the first sub four minute mile in 1954, and in July food rationing in the UK officially ended. Yippee.

Highly significant of course was the release of Rock Around The Clock by Bill Haley & the Comets. Followed in July by the release of That's Alright by

Mablethorpe, 1955.

Jack and Sharon in Mablethorpe in 1955

the unbeatable Elvis Presley on Sun Records. Those two records changed the world.

I don't know what year exactly we got our first television set. It was probably 1954. My first memory of it was sitting on the floor watching The Cisco Kid while a bloke with a large brimmed hat built a new tiled fireplace in our back room. I don't recall if the plumes of dust were from the fireplace man's efforts or from the Cisco Kid's pinto named Diablo kicking up the desert sand as he raced away.

I loved television. I loved films.

On Proctor Place we lived right next door to the local cinema, dislexically spelled Kinema.

The mid-fifties were a time of innocent, adventurous, hero worshipped macho men. My mind became a breeding ground for swashbuckling, gun-slinging, bayonet thrusting warriors. It was good versus evil. Simple, straightforward, no hidden meanings or twisted plots.

My role models were Robin Hood, The Lone Ranger and William Tell.

Ironically nobody ever seemed to get killed. In westerns such as Gunsmoke, Matt Dillon just used to shoot the gun from the baddie's hand without a drop of blood being shed. Robin Hood could fire an arrow in to a villain and he would just fall over shouting... ouch.

Did we ever know the truth about William Tell? How many crossbow bolts did he fire at his son's head before he split the apple? How close were The Lone Ranger and Tonto?

We will never know the answers. We now live in a totally different world... and I don't mean different from the 12th century. I mean different in all ways from the 1950s. Heroes are now replaced by anti heroes, and being a baddie can make you streetwise depending usually how cool you and your clothes are.

American imports on our TV screens in those days were Lassie, I Love Lucy, Dragnet and more. All pretty much innocent. Good job we didn't get all their TV during that time though. Apparently there was a really big show on Stateside called Leave it to Beaver. I bet they didn't show that in the Bible belt.

I don't suppose I could read too well until I was five. Because of that I didn't always know what films were on during any week next door at the Kinema.

Many of them would have been A or X rated fims. A films was the rating where any child under the age of 15 had to be accompanied by an adult. X films were usually "scary" type science fiction films or films showing a hint of female cleavage. No children at all - accompanied or not - could get to see an X rated film.

In later years me and my friend Michael B would ask any adult entering the cinema "to take us in to see an A film". If they said "yes", we would pass the shilling to the adult who would then pay for us. Imagine the uproar nowadays.? Newspaper headlines - "PERVERT TAKES MONEY OFF CHILDREN FOR DODGY FILM", or on adult and paying children watching a James Dean film - "FUMBLE WITHOUT A CAUSE".

No wonder the Playstation and X Box were invented. It was a Government plot to keep kids out of cinemas.

If I had been of age during that period I could have seen such greats as Creature From The Black Lagoon, On The Waterfront, The Searchers, East Of Eden and Giant. The last two being James Dean's other films apart from the aforementioned Fumble.

My mum and dad did take me to see Bridge On The River Kwai however. The scene where Alec Guiness is locked

Jack with Mum and dad, Skegness 1956

in the little tin hut is most disturbing and I feel sure it started the onset of my lifelong claustrophobia. Good old Alec.

One 1955 film I never saw at the Kinema is the utterly immense Love Is A Many Splendoured Thing starring William Holden and Jennifer Jones. Of course I have seen it since and admire not just the film, but it's powerful and haunting theme tune.

The mid 1950s were a great time for innovation and invention.

In 1955 fish fingers were on sale for the very first time. What a simple and remarkable way to eat fish. Kids could now eat fish without greasy, smelly pieces of skin attached. Birds Eye produced them from their factory in Great Yarmouth. Over 600 tons of the product was sold in the first year alone. Still a great favourite today, fish fingers have a wildly nostalgic value and they're a simple recipe to feed hungry kids as well as faddy, squeamish kids like I used to be.

A couple of years further on and another fantastic invention hit the scene; The Hula Hoop. In 1957-1958 everyone I knew had one. Mine was orange ribbed plastic and I loved it. The name Hula Hoop came from the Hawaiian dance that resembled the movement needed to keep the hoop in motion. The product, marketed by the founders WHAM-O, sold 25 million hoops worldwide in two months.

The Soviet Union said the hula hoop was an example of "the emptiness of American culture". So what I ask? All the kids in the Western world were having a great time. Nothing wrong with that.

I must have been around the age of three-and-a-half, maybe just approaching four. My father had taken me out one Sunday lunchtime to meet a friend of his in a Working Men's Club in the Netherthorpe area of Sheffield. He was only in the club around 10 minutes or so, and I had to sit outside on the steps. I must have been thinking "I'm gonna get him back for this," and I did.

Near to the club was a tiny toy shop showing in its window marbles, Dinky Toys, plastic soldiers and tennis balls. The crowning glory however was a Davy Crockett hat (coonskin cap) laid open in its box showing all its luxurious fur and its elegant red silk inner lining.

The cap had been popularised by a Davy Crockett television special made by Disney. I don't remember seeing this Disney special but I do remember all the kids around our way wearing a Crockett cap.

As we walked back from the club towards the shop I recall squeezing my dad's hand and leading him towards the shop window.

"I want a Davy Crockett cap ."

"You're not having one."

"I want one. I want one. Buy me one."

"No we're going home." At this point I started to cry and scream and stamp my feet.

"Get me one. Get me one. Get me one".

"Wait there." I knew I'd won.

"Here, and don't ever ask me for anything else."

He pushed the box in to my chest. Hurriedly I opened the box, took out the cap and marvelled at its incredible workmanship. It felt like nothing I would ever touch again until I was 15. The serene red silk inner added to the cap gave a sublime feeling of luxury.

I stuffed the cap on my head, gave the box to my dad and strode hand in hand with him proudly to the tram stop.

In the years of 1954-1955 the U.S. manufacturer realised $300 million in sales. That equates to $2.6 billion in 2016. That's a lot of coonskin. This one product in itself in those two years outsold anything Elvis and the Beatles would do later.

In those days we had a car. It was a Wolseley. I can't remember what model it was but it was quite big and had a running board like a gangster's car. We had a name for the car. Nellybelle. Now I believe she got her name from us copying the name of the jeep in the Roy Rogers TV show of the fifties. Difference was that true Nellybelle was a jeep. The name stuck for our Wolseley however, and I think she ran well for two or three years until finally giving up the ghost probably in 1959.

Two incidents I remember well about the car. I guess it must have been 1957/58 as my dad was driving up Woodland Street towards my grandparents' house in Channing Street. A black and white collie sprinted from the front door of a terraced house straight in to our path. My dad hit the brakes... hard. In those days cars didn't have seatbelts and I was propelled from the back seat on to the front wooden dashboard. Blood everywhere. My top lip had burst open and panic ensued. I was rushed in to the nearest house for attention. Mrs. Coates I believe was the householder's name. Anyway she ran two towels under the cold water tap and within minutes both had turned fully crimson. I remember people kept checking my teeth but they were all there.

"They're his milk teeth aren't they?"

"Not all of them. Some are second teeth." I heard.

"He needs stitches", someone pointed out. I shook my head violently, not wanting stitches. Blood splattered everywhere like a scene from Scarface.

"Six or seven stitches I reckon," claimed a voice. More head shaking from me, and more blood dispersing randomly.

"Jackie, we're taking you to the Childrens Hospital."

"Dough you're dot", I replied through the blood soaked towels.
"It wain't hurt, honest."

By now Mrs Coates room was like a crowded courtroom. All the street had turned out.

Meanwhile, the collie was probably with some mongrel bitch having fun in somebody's outside toilet.

My dad spoke out: "He's not going to hospital. It'll heal itself. If he says he won't have it stitched then he won't. It will heal."

"Thank God for that", I thought.

Around the same time, maybe a few months later, Nellybelle took us to Skegness for the day. On the way back home, and as the light was beginning to fade (must have been late August), the roof blew off the car. Yes, the roof. I remember being quite amused by it. I also remember that I was wearing a false plastic moustache, round black plastic false glasses and a set of goofy teeth.

My mum turned to me and smiled as my dad brought the car to a halt. He examined the damage and raced across the road to a small farmhouse. He returned with a hammer and a handful of tacks. You see the roof wasn't made of metal. Oh no, it was a type of canvas it seemed.

He tapped away for a while until finally declaring us roadworthy again. He returned the hammer and thanked the farmer endlessly before starting the engine, and heading for home at a snail's pace.

Now, you can imagine this happening to a driver in Tornado Alley on the Great Plains, but not in the passive, docile countryside that is Lincolnshire. Anyway, it happened to us, and I remember arriving back home on Proctor Place still sucking away on my goofy teeth, keenly awaiting the next adventure.

As a postscript to all this, just a few weeks after my ghastly lip injury, I was playing in the yard at home with neighbours Philip and Roy. We were playing a version of hockey with a golf ball and broomstick handles. Philip swung his broomstick lustily and it came down upon my top lip. As if that wasn't enough, the broomstick had a nail through it and that ripped open my previous wound. Blood everywhere again, and more threats of stitches and hospitals. Luckily, I got away with it... again.

So, as a consequence of those long summer days of the fifties I have carried a scar shaped like a small arrowhead on my top lip. It's a little bit like a hare lip but a much smaller version, and unlike a hare lip it has never impeded my speech.

Woodland Street no longer exists. Mrs Coates will have passed on years ago and hopefully the collie will have fornicated himself into an early grave.

Chapter Three
Hit the road Jack (1958-1962)

"Jackie, Jackie. Come here a minute. I want you to run me an errand."

When I was 9 or 10 years-old I would often hear that call. I would hear it on Friday lunchtime especially during the school holidays. It was our next door neighbour, Mrs. Lee.

"Yes Mrs. Lee?" I would ask upon entering her door.

"Jackie, I want you to go across to the fish shop and ask Mr. Burrows if he has got a nice tail end for me."

Of course she did mean tailend of cod but, in my innocence, I would repeat her request to Mr. Burrows time after time. I remember asking one particular Friday and a group of Teddy boys were laughing at me. I hadn't a clue of course what the great joke was.

Only in later years did I catch on and, by then, Mrs. Lee had sadly passed away and the love of tailends had passed with her.

I never liked Teddy boy types. My dad and grandad took me on a fishing trip in to Lincolnshire one Sunday when I was maybe only 8. Mid-morning and we were in a café in Sleaford having stopped for a breakfast on the way to the Boston area. Some Teds were gathered around a juke box. I walked over to see what they were up to. A rock'n'roll record came on and they started moving arms, hands and feet to the beat. I was too near to them. One Ted shot out his elbow in his dance and caught me full in the eye.

"You alright kid?", he enquired. I nodded and walked away, my eye puffing up and streaming uncontrollably.

My grandad noticed my plight and cried out, "reight, I'm gonna sort yor lot out" (and he would have). My dad had to forcibly restrain him. Consequently, I've never liked Teddy boys, or their girlfriends with hair that looked like candy floss. Still, they will all be at least 75-years-old now, so I'd better shut up.

Other groups of people were beginning to appear around that time. Noticeably the beatniks. Now around working class Sheffield 6 you didn't see too many of them. You were lucky to see any adult not wearing a flat cap for instance. Well, the women of course didn't wear flat caps. They usually wore headscarves.

Chiffon headscarves being particularly popular, unless of course you were in middle age, and you would wear silky ones, very often with prints of royalty and pageantry on them.

Anyway, the odd beatnik appeared here and there, and always stood out in a crowd for being different. They would often wear a beret, a turtleneck sweater and dark glasses. A goatee beard would be worn, but only usually by the men. They used words such as square, cat, cool and dig. They used to dig modern jazz.

You could say beatniks were forerunners of the late sixties hippies. They were liberals, left wing and anti war, just as hippies

Jack on horseback, with Shirley and Philip Swift. He still has the horse

purported to be a few years later. Beatniks and hippies preached the rejection of materialism. This is what happens when people adapt pseudo intellectualism. They think they have all the answers, but in fact are only usually half educated, and just like to be seen as being different.

It doesn't last forever. At some stage people need to eat, to be sheltered, to be loved, to be cared for, and to procreate. Money is needed. Nobody can live a lifetime on ideals.

Britain is a society built on different class levels. I have very rarely met anyone from the working classes who felt the need to be a beatnik or hippy. This is why a few years later the mod movement came in to being. Mod represented smart young working class people who dressed well and openly flaunted materialism. "Clean living under difficult circumstances", was their slogan.

Back in the fifties we also had something very different to cope with. The weather. Fog was the thing I remember most. From October to January it was always around. I did love the fog though. You could hide in it, take a ride in it, sit outside in it, commit suicide in it. I remember November evenings when the moon was bright orange. That was probably because of the chemicals from the steelworks filling the sky with liberal portions of sulphur, phosphorus, chromium and various other potential killer metals and gases. Kids were outside all the time in those days and nobody gave a thought to air pollution or namby pamby stuff like that. Toxins? We chewed on them like sweets.

History records that 1959 was a very warm, dry summer and it certainly does strike me that in my memory the summers I lived through as a little kid were always much drier and sunnier than the so called summers of the sixties.

Snow always seemed thicker and deeper then, and the ice stayed around for weeks. Schools didn't shut then either. If it snowed really heavily, then you still went to school. The teachers would be there, so you had to be there.

The Kinema was so busy during these years with a whole host of fantastic films, many of which are still labelled as classic to this day.

1958 gave us; Vertigo, South Pacific, The Vikings, Inn of the Sixth Happiness.

1959; Ben Hur, Rio Bravo, North by North West, Some like it Hot.

1960; Psycho, Spartacus, The Alamo, Magnificent Seven.

1961; West Side Story, The Comancheros, The Hustler, Breakfast at Tiffanys.

What a great era for film. Of course at my very tender age I didn't see too many of these films, but I did see G.I.Blues with Elvis Presley and the delectable Juliet Prowse. Even at the age of 9 she made me feel uncomfortable.

In the early sixties the world had plenty to be scared of. Not just ordinary scared like when you ride on a ghost train, or see a spider or something. No, really scared, indeed petrified.

It was almost like the night I had a dream about Gloria Gaynor. I dreamed she was sitting at the bottom of my bed. Well, first I was afraid, then I was petrified... Any way, real fear.

The Cuban missile crisis of 1962 was terrifying for all. Mostly we kids. The United States and the Soviet Union threatened each other daily. Neither side would back down.

Men wearing trilbys and raincoats manned street corners carrying banners, proclaimed that "the end was nigh". How nigh could it be? I thought kids being kids we didn't think about it, but we did. I had only ever heard the word nigh in one context previously. This was when older people, grandparents mostly, would comment that so and so at number 15, or her who works in't bread shop must be "nigh on 60 if she's a day".

Well to me at such an age as I was, I reckoned that anybody as nigh to death as nearly 60 shouldn't be around anyway and they wouldn't be missed at all if an H bomb landed on their skull. Which again makes me wonder if anybody has ever been hit full on the cranium by an H bomb, A bomb or anything that the Luftwaffe had ever dropped.

My worst experience during this period was equally as traumatic as being hit on the head by a bomb. It was as fraught with calamity as meeting up with Fidel Castro in a dark alley.

You see living at that time as we did on Proctor Place, we had a dear old outside toilet. Also, because toilet paper was not widely used by the general populace, especially the working class variety, newspaper was used as a wiping device.

So, one day at school as we were all getting changed for P.E, I noticed a lad in my class staring keenly at my bottom.

"What you looking at?" I asked.

"I see Kennedy has put a blockade on Cuba", he replied.

Many times after that I noticed kids looking at my arse for football results and the like.

"Can't you get your dad to buy the Green Un?", they would ask.

Or, from the more mature 10-year-olds,"Don't you get Titbits?", which of course was a well established periodical of the time. Titbits? I thought. That's what cats eat.

Sometime during that October the crisis was averted, and the men wearing trilbys took up another cause, on another street corner.

In the summer of that same year, we as a family went to Potter Heigham, Norfolk on holiday for two weeks. My father hired a car. A grey and maroon coloured Ford Anglia. It looked great to me, and I remember looking around Proctor Place to see if anyone was looking as we loaded up the car. Of course nobody was.

It took seven hours to reach our destination. We took the wrong route at Kings Lynn. Altough I didn't know it at the young age of 10, in order to reach the Norfolk Broads, you should head for Norwich, and thereafter it's relatively easy.

We didn't head for Norwich, but instead drifted northwards towards the

24

North Norfolk coast, and took in such delights as Sandringham, Hunstanton, Wells next the sea, Marston and Sheringham.

Eventually, somehow we arrived at Acle. God knows how we got there but we did. Spotting an agricultural type, my father brought the car to a halt, wound down the window and enquired of him the way to Potter Heigham. The local replied something like "aaarrrgh, be it that way", as his rudden face beamed and great globules of sweat poured down his smiling face. For months after I kept repeating the immortal phrase "aaaarrrgh be it that way". People kept remarking that I sounded more like Robert Newton as Long John Silver than a farm labourer from the depths of Norfolk.

I didn't care. This bloke was now a hero of mine. I can still see his reddened, balding pate to this day, shining in the late afternoon of this early sixties East Anglian day.

We stayed in the smallest caravan on earth in Potter Heigham. It was the size of an igloo but housed us, uncomfortably for two weeks.

Potter Heigham has a lovely river, the Thurne. Holiday barges and small cruisers still sail it to this day. As much as anything, we were there for the fishing. After my dad had let me join him a couple of times to fish from the river bank, I got in to the habit of walking down there by myself every day with rod, line, and tackle fully assembled.

I caught roach, perch, bream, eels and a few other species of coarse fish. Friendly people waved to me from on board their vessels. Paedophiles hadn't been invented then so I felt perfectly safe.

My favourite record of that period in 1962 was Joe Brown's "Picture of You". I loved that mixture of rock'n'roll, pop and country. I still do to this day. I remember humming it to myself as I cast my line in to the Thurne.

One day in Potter Heigham lives clearly in my memory. It was August 5th, 1962. My dad sent me to the local shop for 20 Park Drive and a newspaper. I chose The Mirror. Walking back to the caravan I read where Marilyn Monroe had been found dead. I found it so hard to take in. How could one so beautiful, famous, talented and blonde just die.? Only people over the age of 60 wearing a flat cap or headscarf died. Nobody who looked like Marilyn ever died.

Sadly not so. I really felt hurt by this news. Picking up my fishing tackle, I walked to the river, and sat fishing for hours trying to comprehend this day of disaster.

Later that year I forgot about Marilyn. Ursula Andress appeared. Living next door to the cinema as we did, the wall outside had a glass frame showing shots of forthcoming feature films. One was Doctor No. Well blow me down, but one of the shots was of Ursula in her part as Honey Rider, walking from the sea and on to the empty beach. It wasn't empty of course because Bond was watching her from behind a palm tree. Lucky James. There was Ursula in her now famous white bikini.

My God, no wonder lads as young as 10 took an interest in the opposite sex so early in those days. She was incredible. I wasn't allowed to pay to watch the film because it was graded A. You had to be accompanied by an adult. So, I had to wait a very tortuous three years until I could see her on the silver screen in "She". Wow she was a goddess in every way. Of course when you are 13 going on 14 you tend to appreciate people's finer points more. Indeed, she really had fine points.

1962 was a very good year for movies. The Kinema showed 300 Spartans and a very British film entitled "It's Trad dad". Now my father was in fact a trad jazz fan."Trad" being short for the word traditional. He used to play records by Chris Barber, Johnnie Dankworth, and Humphrey Lyttleton amongst others. I think he thought I liked jazz too, but he was very wrong. From being six my mother played records for me by Elvis, Lonnie Donegan, Paul Anka, Eddie Cochrane and my taste in music had already been moulded.

Music was just part of my array of interests at that time. A little bit clichéd but I loved sport. Most lads did in those days.

One of the best things I ever witnessed was on a cool July afternoon in 1961. My dad had taken me (after much begging on my part) to the Yorkshire versus Kent cricket fixture at Scarborough. We were on holiday there, and I made him abandon my mother and baby brother Alan for the day.

It was worth it. Batsmen never hit too many sixes in those days. It probably had something to do with the strength of the bats etc. So, when Brian Close launched one that sailed high over our heads at the mid wicket boundary I was dumbstruck. I can still see it clearly in my mind's eye to this day. Brian became my cricketing hero from that moment on.

My football hero was Peter Swan. Tall, strong, commanding, unflappable. Very few got the better of him.

My horse racing hero was the indomitable Lester Piggott. When Lester raised his whip and shook the reins half a furlong from home you just knew the horse would win.

Over and above sport though were my fictional heroes. I never looked at a British comic. I just didn't get excited by them. I did get excited by D.C. Comics however, especially Superman. These comics were incredibly popular. In the U.S.A. in the early sixties, 7 of the top 9 comic titles published featured Superman. Of course Superman did not just feature in his own titled comic, but also in Superboy; Lois Lane; Jimmy Olsen; Action; World's Finest and Adventure. In 1962 in the U.S.A. alone, Superman comics sold 5.9 million copies.

Batman began to catch up in the mid sixties when the TV series began to be shown, (oh, and how good was that by the way? Adam West – fantastic). However the early sixties belonged to Superman. The storylines were, believe it or not, very educational. Much of it was based around science, both fact and fiction. I still believe today, and I mean this, if you can move or travel faster than the speed of light, then you can time travel.

The heroes and villains in the comics were truly goodies and baddies. The heroes were Jimmy Olsen, Lois Lane, the gorgeous Lana Lang. The villains were Lex Luther, Brainiac, Mr. Mxyzptlx, Bizarro and many more. The biggest threat to our superhero was kryptonite however, and his enemies would use it against him at every opportunity.

I just wish I had saved every copy I had ever bought.

Biggles was a fantastic fictional hero for entirely different reasons. James Bigglesworth a.k.a. Biggles was the ultimate adventuring hero of the skies. An intrepid traveller, he sought out and detected scheming, devisive wrongdoers between the two wars after claiming himself 32 kills in fighter planes during the first war. His heroics carried on through World War Two before he became employed as a flying detective for Scotland Yard. A true Brit, Biggles typified the jingoism that we young boys were encouraged to enjoy and engender.

There is no modern day equivalent to Biggles sadly. The best we can do is to give a TV show to Bear Grylls and hope for the best.

Chapter Four
We are family

Mathematician William Shanks (1812-1882) spent the biggest part of his life working out the value of Pi to 707 decimal places. In 1958 an IBM computer did in 40 seconds what Shanks had done in a lifetime. Later in 1995, the billionth digit of Pi was discovered.

My great grandfather, William Byron Watson, was of the same era as Shanks. He was born in Sheffield in 1842 and went on to father several children. My grandfather Hubert was sired by him and born in 1901. William Byron then fathered a further 2 children before he was 70.

Surely this was a far greater accomplishment than sitting down all day with a pencil scribbling away at long division to prove just what? He would have been much better sireing children, because one day one of the children might, just might, earn him and the whole family a lot of money.

I suppose though it was easy for William Byron. His wife (that is his second wife and my great grandmother) was named Fanny. That must have given him a head start. Well maybe not the head, but something anatomical.

It must have been the love of cattle and breeding that drove the Watsons to reproduce. My grandad Hubert married Adelaide Rose Shaw in the early 1920s. They had 5 children, eldest of which was my father, Jack. He had a brother and three sisters - Dennis, Adelaide, Margaret, and Carole.

Now, I know I am biased, immensely so. However, the aforesaid group of people, apart from William and Fanny who I never met, have all played an enormous part in influencing my life from a very young age.

My grandmother encouraged me to read all the same books she had read as a small girl. Treasure Island, Kidnapped, Catriona, and the Master of Ballantrae. All written of course by the enormously gifted Robert Louis Stevenson. Stevenson's mother by the way was also named Fanny. There was a lot if it about in those days it seems.

My grandad Hubert talked to me of cattle, and horse racing, of football and cricket. He talked of boxing champions from the 1920s and 1930s. People such as Tommy Farr, and Jack Dempsey. He also talked of his dislike for Sheffield United and Surrey cricket.

He never changed his views. If he had a dislike for something or somebody, then that was it for life.

Nobody ever called him Hubert. He was always known as Son to everyone, even my grandmother. I now have a grandson called Sonny, I am so proud to say. Also, a grandson named William carrying forward the name of his great, great, great grandfather born in 1842. William was born in 2012, 170 years later. You can't put a price on that.

In 1874 in Somersham, Suffolk, just 5 miles from Ipswich a baby boy was born with the name of Edgar in to the Bowers family. Brought up in a farm labouring community Edgar was ambitious for a more challenging, more rewarding, better paid future. So, at some point in the 1890s he left his rural home and set out for the rapidly expanding northern industrial city of Sheffield where you could, it was rumoured, make a fortune, or die of tuberculosis in advance of that fortune.

He lived, married, and fathered four children.

One of these offspring was my maternal grandfather Edgar Askew Bowers, born 1902. Edgar Askew married his sweetheart Ethel Green in the early 1920s, and they quickly became parents to four children within a few years.

My mother Doris (Dolly) was born in January 1928. Her elder sister Edna was born in 1924, her younger sister Ethel in 1931. However, the first born was a boy named Jack who only lived for 2 years or so, and died sadly of an abdominal complication. Apparently it is said that for some reason my grandad blamed himself for young Jack's death, and carried the torment of this tragedy with him to his own grave.

My grandmother Ethel was a quiet, nervy woman who I remember being admitted to hospital for a variety of complaints. She had as a young woman in 1918 contracted the pandemic Spanish flu, and this had seemingly left her weakened for life. This deadly strain spread rapidly around the world, and infected 500 million people it is estimated. It has been labelled "the greatest medical holocaust in history", and may have killed more people than the Black Death. 17 million in India alone died from the virus.

Ethel was born the eldest of 13 children. Brought up in a 2 up, 2 down in Walkley,

Jack's grandma in the 1920s

Ethel Bowers

Grandma and Grandad Watson, Fleetwood, 1964

she survived the Spanish flu, had 4 children herself, and although suffering the after effects of the lethal virus toughed it out until her death in 1967.

When I was perhaps 4-years-old my mother would take me to Channing Street visiting her mother, my grandma. My mother and her 2 sisters would gather around a wooden table and chat with their mother about all the local goings on. If they thought it was something I shouldn't know about they would all speak very quietly or mime words and actions.

I once recall my grandma telling her daughters that her across the road at number 119 "had all took". This produced gasps and sighs from the daughters. I felt sorry for the poor woman at 119 as well because I thought she had been burgled. In a strange sort of way, I suppose she had been burgled. Somebody had nicked her uterus. She had a hysterectomy.

As I remember nobody ever gave my grandma enough credit for her life. I hope that these few lines will help correct that. Just one more thing. Only recently have I

Grandad Watson in the early 1960s

been lucky enough to view a photograph of her when young. She was an incredibly good looking woman. Well done Ethel, and thank you for being you.

So, the Watson/Bowers connection was all primed and ready to roll. In 1942 my mother, Dolly, and my father Jack crossed each other's paths. I really don't know how the story developed but in November 1945 they married. Dolly was two months short of 18, and Jack was 20. By all accounts it was a bit of a rushed affair. Nothing shotgun about it because I wasn't due to be born for another six years.

Jack's dad in uniform

It seems that my dad had been conscripted in to the R.A.F. and was due to be sent overseas to India and the Far East. They decided to marry before he went in order to form a bond that would endure through and beyond the 2 years' national service. I have a wonderful coloured framed copy of the wedding photo, and my mother looks fabulous in her wedding dress, while my father looks strikingly handsome in his blue R.A.F. uniform.

I was so fortunate to have these people as my parents. They were modern, forward thinking, yet down to earth and understanding of all my many needs as a small child.

My father, for a fleeting moment, in May 1953 became a local celebrity after winning the Sheffield "Star Walk", a road walking race over approximately 12.5 miles up and over the many hills of our city. In second place was my

Jack's Dad on the way to victory in the 1953 Star Walk

Jack's dad wins The Star Walk

uncle John, husband to my mother's youngest sister Ethel. As with all outdoor sporting events during that era tens of thousands of people turned out along the route to cheer the competitors on. I still have black & white photos of the day.

Athletics was a big thing for my dad. He had won many medals in the R.A.F. for his 440 yards running as well as high jump and long jump. After leaving the forces he competed in local weekend events in 100, 220, and 440 yards racing. Our house was stacked full of medals, cups, diplomas, rosettes and a wide variety of household goods given as prizes.

One sunny afternoon when I was five, he entered me in to the kids' 50 yard dash at his works sports day. Against six or seven other kids I strode away and won. I wish I hadn't. At the prize presentation in a large marquee in front of hundreds of people the announcer declared Jackie Watson as the winner of the kids 50 yard dash. I walked to the stage glowing with pride. The announcer looking puzzled passed me my prize. It was a spinning Cinderella doll. I always hated being called Jackie after that. I suppose my dad was getting his own back for the Davy Crockett cap episode.

His other great motivation was trade unionism and politics. I don't know quite what got him started with the trade union movement, but when I was a kid he was always at meetings of the local branch of the Boilermakers & Blacksmiths Union. Eventually he got to be the head of the movement in our area.

He became from that position a very active member of the Labour Party. So much so that in May 1969 he was elected as the city councillor for Owlerton ward, a safe Labour stronghold.

During the seventies, he was at one point deputy leader of Sheffield City Council and chairman of the parks and recreation committee.

He was very well known throughout the city, and although he died at a relatively young age, many people said that in his 54 years on planet earth he had lived such a full life that it may just as well have been 80.

My mother was an incredible woman. She taught me to read, and taught me to walk straight and upright "like a soldier". She taught me to love rock'n'roll. However, she struggled to teach me how to behave when going in to school. I acted horribly and would try every method known to man to avoid entering Malin Bridge infants school of a morning. She suffered two years of that bad behaviour from me, but kept her patience and always gave me encouragement. I was a proper little horror but she endured the ordeal until I finally surrendered, and head down entered the school reluctantly but peacefully every day. All I ever got from my mother was praise and support. She never put me down. She did everything for me and my father. She washed for us, cooked for us, baked for us, ironed for us and much, much, more. Her selflessness was second to none.

In November 1960, she gave birth to Alan, and then there were four of us in our old, decaying (but not neglected) Victorian terrace. The arrival of Alan just served to accelerate her work ethic, and within a few weeks she was doing everything for us including washing dozens of nappies each week in an old twin tub washer. No disposables in those days of course. All nappies were terry towelling and the challenge was to get them all gleaming white to hang on your washing line. No self-respecting housewife would dare show her face to the neighbours if a hint of grey was apparent.

When in 1965 we moved to Liberty Hill (more of that later), my mother's work rate accelerated even more. The new maisonette was pristine but needed upkeep and she got stuck in to the task daily. Not only that, but she took on two cleaning jobs to help pay the weekly rent. My clothes were always washed and ironed ready for school day in, day out. She even polished my shoes. How she kept up the momentum I will never know. She was relentless, and would simply never allow

Jack's mum in the late 1940s

33

me, Alan or my father to do anything within the house. I cannot imagine any woman alive in the western world of today sacrificing themselves in such a way to the needs of their family. God bless her. We all loved her so much.

15th November 1960 was as I recall a very foggy affair and typical of our city in that month and in that era. Me and my father were staying at my grandma's house on Balmain Road, Sutton Estate. I was told that my mother was in confinement, and that I shouldn't worry. Confinement? Surely that was the same as being imprisoned I thought.

My dad had gone to the hospital to see what was happening, and about 5pm my grandma gave me a few pennies to go to the phone box near the Bee Hive pub. My instructions were to ask politely how Mrs. Watson was progressing and just when the baby might be born.

"Mrs. Watson has had her baby. She has a baby boy, and you have a baby brother". For a minute, I thought she had given birth to 2 boys judging by the way I was informed.

"Oh, thank you, thank you". I put down the receiver, escaped from the phone box, and raced back to 51 Balmain Road. I burst through the kitchen door where my grandma sat, cup of tea in hand. "She has had a boy. My mother has had a boy", I shouted excitedly.

"Oh, that's good news Jackie. A little boy," she replied. "Is your mum alright?"

Jack with brother Alan – Fleetwood in 1964

"I think so. I never asked."

"Oh, I'm sure she will be. Did you get any change from the phone box?"

"Yes, two pence," I replied as I placed it on the kitchen table.

"Well you keep that, and buy yourself some sweets on the way to school tomorrow".

I pushed the change in to my shorts and figured I'd get some sherbet dabs. I really liked those.

It was days and days before my mother came home out of hospital. She arrived eventually with my dad and my new baby brother at Balmain Road.

Everybody was saying "oooh, isn't he lovely Dolly?" and "can I hold him for a bit?" Some pushed sixpences in his hand. That bit seemed to work. He has never been short of money since that day.

So, back on Proctor Place there were now 4 of us, plus the cat of course. My job was to fetch baby Alan's tinned oster milk from the Co-Op on Middlewood Road. I didn't get involved with anything else. I was 9 for Christ's sake I didn't want to be involved with feeding or nappies or washing things. I remember nappies being washed and dried constantly, and there was a sort of thin rainbow of moisture hovering around the room we all lived in, cooked in, ate in, watched television in, fed the cat in.

Alan grew strong and fine and resembled the Hubert (grandfather) side of the family with his sandy/fair hair and many freckles. He had a real temper and no matter how many times you hit him, he always came back for more. I suppose that goes with the colouring.

From a very young age he took an interest in football and cricket, and practically taught himself to read by studying the Sheffield Green Un from front to back at the age of 5. At 6 years old he was with us all as 18,000 Wednesdayites travelled to Stamford Bridge for a sixth-round F.A Cup tie, and sang heartily with everyone else to the chanted lyrics of "Bollocks to Chelsea."

Alan excelled at school at most subjects and was always enthusiastic in any form of competition or sport. He always wanted to win. If he didn't win he would mount an attack, usually if I scored a last-minute winner at Subbuteo and then began to exaggerate my celebration.

When he was 2 months short of the age of 9, and I was 18, I left him and my parents for the beginning of a life elsewhere. On the same morning, my mother said to me "You don't have to get married today. You can call it off." That was the mark of a woman in my opinion who truly loved her family. Sadly, I was too drunk to give her an answer.

Chapter Five
From a Jack to A King (1963)

B efore embarking on the writing of this chapter, and in the course of doing a little research, I stumbled across something rather coincidental.

Anita Ekberg was incredibly beautiful, as were many of her contemporaries from that era. There must have been something in the water back in the 1920s and 1930s to make so many gorgeous females be born upon the planet in such a short space of time. However, I had never known the fact that she married an actor by the name of Rik Van Nutter. The year was 1963.

Why would you marry a nutter? Presumably she became Mrs. Nutter. She was certainly the best-looking nutter I've ever seen. Not only that, but checking Rik's details on Wikipedia, it transpires that his real name was actually Frederick Allen Nutter. My late father in law (God rest his soul) had the name of Frederick Allen. I thank my lucky stars that during the time that I knew him I did not know that the lovely Anita had married F.A.Nutter.

If I had known during my in-law Fred's lifetime then I would, during a drunken hour in his presence I'm sure, have used the full name to take the piss. That could have been curtains for me. Great bloke as my father in-law was, he would not have stood to be ridiculed. I would have risked it for Anita though.

I have heard it said that until 1963 Great Britain was still a nation gripped by the legacy of Victorian doctrine and principle. 1963 changed virtually everything in this country. We moved up a gear.

Many factors were involved in this change . Growing optimism from boomers was beginning to seep through to those born 1946-1948 who were now earning wages and had money to spend. Clothes, music, patterns of thought were all about to change rapidly, and good old traditional values were about to be challenged and altered for ever.

So much changed that year. For me, having followed cricket so closely for 4 years and more, I was used to the slow, thought out batting of teams, and the gradual building of innings on docile English pitches. Then the West Indies arrived. They were a revelation. I had never seen anybody, Brian Close apart, attack a cricket ball quite like they did.

Butcher, Hunte, Kanhai and the fantastic Garfield Sobers all put the English bowlers to the sword. Only Fred Trueman stood up to them. Then when they came out to bowl they had the aggressive Hall and Griffiths in their armoury. England had in their side Dexter, Cowdrey and Close, but they struggled particularly against Griffiths who had 12 months previously finished a batsman's career by fracturing his skull. Charlie took 32 wickets in the 5 match series for an average of 16.21. The West Indies won the series 3-1. Charlie was portrayed to us all as a nasty, evil villain, but by all accounts, he was a really nice gentle bloke. He just played to win.

Playing to win is the only way. I always wanted to win, and hated losing. Although I had no great love of learning by any means I was good at English, arithmetic, geography, history and to supplement this, for the last two years at Malin Bridge junior school we had the superb Mr. Lewis Hawley as teacher.

Mr. Hawley primed our class of 50 in to getting an eleven plus pass. His teaching methods were tried and tested and our results as a group from that class were excellent. I can't remember the figures but, I reckon a good 70% of the 50 passed to grammar schools. 8 of we boys passed to King Edward VII grammar school, the top school in Yorkshire probably at that time.

We took the eleven plus exams in school over three test papers. English, arithmetic, and aptitude. It was February and freezing cold. January, February and early March of that year according to the Central England temperature record was the third coldest Winter ever on record after 1683-84 and 1739-40.

Regardless of that we had to get to school to take the exams. Three separate papers over three days as the snow and ice grew thicker outside. I recall before one of these exams, a bench dropped right across my toes leaving them all bruised and bleeding, and throbbing for days. I limped home through the ice in my short trousers (no boy wore long trousers even in the coldest winter since 1740.) Girls didn't wear trousers either. It was unheard of. Skirts were the order of the day.

One Saturday morning in June 1963 I was awakened by my mother with the results of the exams.

"You've not passed and you're only going to Wisewood school." she said sternly.

"Oh, that's alright. I'm not bothered anyway", came my answer.

"No, just kidding. You've passed and you've been given a place at King Edward."

I didn't know whether to laugh or cry. My life would be changing from September and I knew it. I got a £1 note for my good exam result, and

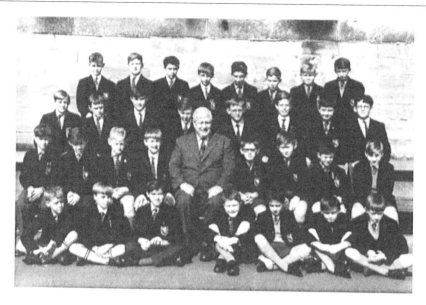

Form 1(1) 1963/64

Richard Russell, Keith Whittles, John Sampson, Nick Mines, John Harker, Chris Naylor, Gerry Hargon, Richard Thomas,
R "Brunner" Brown, Andrew Peterkin, Steve Gillam, J A "Masher" McKenna, Glyn Jones, Paul Jay, Simon Childs, Paul Cook,
John Walker, Jack Watson, Stuart Rotherham, Nigel D C Clark, Mr H T R Twyford, John Addy, David Belton, Rudi Lutz, Ron Proctor,
Nigel Hoskison, Mick Nichols, Richard Sorsby, Roger Howard, Malcolm Fowles (one of twins), Willy Wallis, Andrew Lynn (one of twins).

Photo • names courtesy of Richard Thomas

I tucked it away safely knowing that in a few week's time we would be on holiday in Caistor, near Great Yarmouth.

Shortly afterwards I achieved something I got more of a buzz from than passing an exam. I swam my 25 yards' length and got my certificate for it. I had been trying in hourly sessions once a week from September 1962 to get this certificate. God knows it had been hard. For a start, I was a complete novice. My mother had always discouraged me from going to the swimming baths. She said people caught polio there. Not just in Hillsborough baths of course but in all public swimming baths.

Not only that but the baths were teaming with people who were really good swimmers. Then there was me. A fragile figure in red trunks milling around with a polystyrene board in front of me. I must have looked a complete idiot. I did persist though despite my fears and inhibitions. Finally, I said to the swimming teacher who used to talk to us in a very slow monotone voice, "can I swim this length from the deep end to the shallow end instead of the other way round?"

She looked at me as if I was retarded, and must have thought, "not only is this kid stupid, he's also bleedin suicidal."

"I don't see why not", she replied with a worried look on her face.

It made sense to me. My train of thought was that if I could survive the first 10-12 yards, which I knew I was just about capable of, then if I felt I was struggling, at least it wouldn't be as easy to drown as the pool became shallower. I hope that makes sense!

So, I pushed off from the deep end, and the monotone teacher held a wooden pole in to the water just below my chin.

"It's going well", I thought as I just about reached halfway. I wish she would shift that pole it's getting in my way."

10 yards from the shallow end and kids were splashing each other, fighting, cavorting, blocking my route.

"Come on Jackie, nearly there", cried Miss Monotone.

"Shift those kids" I thought, "oh, and that frigging pole".

Two yards to go and I lunged towards the wall, finishing in style like Mark Spitz would do some years later. I wanted to punch the air and hug the teacher. It would have been rather inappropriate considering I was wearing only a pair of skimpy red trunks however.

She said, "well done" and walked off away from me. What a bitch! There was I looking for pats on the back, and awaiting hearty hugs in front of tv cameras, and all I got was "well done". I didn't even get "for he's a jolly good fellow" from my school friends who were obviously disinterested in my success.

I dreamed of the Olympic pool. The glamour and glittering of gold. Maybe Tokyo would come too soon, but who knows Mexico in 1968 was only five years away.

A lot of water was to pass under the bridge in those five years 1963-1968. Unfortunately, an Olympic swimmer I never became. 1963 was a very, very big year though, and a lot was to happen before the end of it.

In early 1963, the Beatles finished playing the Star Club in Hamburg. Returning to Britain, they released "Please Please Me", and never looked back. What was to happen over the next few months affected everyone. Here was something completely different. Between January and September that fated year they had appeared many times on television, conducted their first British tour, reached number 1 with "Please Please Me" and "She Loves You", released both singles in the U.S.A., released their first album, and led the way for others to follow.

Billy J. Kramer and the Dakotas, Gerry and the Pacemakers, and the

Searchers all stormed their way to success as they followed in the wake of the Beatles.

I began to grow my hair foregoing the Brylcreemed, neat combing effect. On my form school photo in September 1963 my face could barely be seen because of the hair above it. Musically I still searched for something else however. I had always liked Chuck Berry and still listened to him. It wouldn't be until the next year when stuff I really, really liked began to come through.

So, in July 1963 I said my farewell to Malin Bridge School. It was a warm, sunny day, and I recall turning around to look at it again as I walked away down Meredith Road.

The next day we were off on holiday for two weeks. This time to Caistor-On-Sea, near Great Yarmouth. We took the train this time though, and I remember the four of us (Alan being only two-and-a-half) being seated in one of those old-fashioned carriages with doors on that seated six or so.

Unlike our 1962 caravan hire in Potter Heigham, this caravan was modern and spacious, and the site had several amenities, notably a milk vending machine which had cartons, the likes of which I had never seen before. As far as I knew milk only came in glass bottles. I think it was one shilling per carton, and I bought at least one on a daily basis, just for the hell of it. Mind you, trying to undo the carton to fit it between your lips was a nightmare.

Each day we were there I hired one of those go-kart shaped vehicles with four wheels, but simply pedal power, no engine. I loved it. Just cruising the paths between the caravans, peddling and steering away, making out I was in Southern California. Well I wasn't I was on the North Sea coast. Still, with your hands on a steering wheel, and swigging on a cool milk carton as the sun is going down, who gives a damn.? The future could wait. My new school included. Who wants to be an academic anyway? I would sooner be a beach boy.

On 10th August we were aboard the train on our way home. It must have been 3pm when my dad said "put the news on the light programme Jack." I switched the dial on my fabulous Bush transistor radio to the BBC light programme.

A really well-spoken, solemn voice was giving details of a crime that had occurred that would later be called "The Great Train Robbery". A train travelling from Glasgow to Euston on the morning of 8th August had been held up by 15 robbers and emptied of its £2.6million cargo. This vast sum was stored in £1 and £5 banknotes, and was the then equivalent of £49 million in 2016.

This of course was massive news at the time, especially seeing as the establishment had had its arse well and truly kicked. The news dragged on about this crime for months, indeed years if I'm truthful. In fact it was never truly put to bed until the death of anti-hero Ronnie Biggs in 2013. I didn't think it was such big news at the time. I had been watching trains getting held up on screen in the Kinema for years. In the old wild west of course. So, nothing new "just get on with it," I thought.

More frightening news was that in the Far East people were dying from immolating themselves. Well I had heard that it could turn you blind, but to just go up in smoke, keel over and die? They must have been doing it all too quickly. I made a mental note to watch out for that in future.

The last quarter of 1963 saw some particularly terrifying life changing events. On 23rd November Doctor Who was shown on BBC for the very first time. Starring William Hartnell as the Doctor, nobody had quite seen or heard anything that could compare to it previously. Here was a man who lived, worked, travelled inside a police box. As my grandad commented at the time, "What a load of bollocks".

In truth, it was not so much the storylines or the characters that startled everyone. My God, no. After all, most people had previously watched Quatermass. No, it was the theme music that startled adults, and scared little children.

"Dum di dum, dum di dum, dum di dum, der der" it went. The main bass line rhythm was recorded from a single plucked string played over and over again, then mixed and churned out by electronic synthesiser. Even now ask anyone the theme tune and immediately they will go in to "dum di dum, dum di dum etc...". Frightening as it may have been to some, it all paled in to insignificance with the news from Dallas, Texas the previous day. 22nd November had all started very much like any ordinary November day. The Beatles second album, "With the Beatles" was released that same Friday and because of their immense popularity and pre-ordered bookings for the record it was an immediate smash hit here in Britain.

Aldous Leonard Huxley, the English writer, novelist, and philosopher passed away that Friday. Famous for his book "The Doors of Perception", it recalls experiences when taking a psychedelic drug. His legacy was not just having the book name adapted as the stage name for my favourite ever band, "The Doors", but also for his life as a humanist, pacifist and satirist. His influence over the young generation would be felt more and more in the coming years.

The news that staggered the planet that day was the untimely, premature death of John F. Kennedy. The assassination of the most prominent human being on the planet stunned all.

I remember the moment I heard the news. It was Friday evening and I was doing my history homework. There was a special announcement on BBC television. My father looked at me, my mother and my 3-year-old brother Alan. Nobody spoke. For the rest of the evening the television was filled with the detail of the horrific news.

70 minutes after the shooting Lee Harvey Oswald was arrested for the murder of JFK. Oswald had also shot police officer Tippit before his arrest. Oswald's case never came to trial. Two days later while being escorted to a car for transfer at Dallas police headquarters, Oswald himself was shot dead. The perpetrator was Jack Ruby, a night club owner. The scene was filmed live on American television.

Just two hours after the President's death, Lyndon B. Johnson was sworn in as U.S. president. Jackie Kennedy, the dead president's wife is photographed beside Johnson as he takes the oath. Despite all her trauma Mrs. Kennedy appears disturbingly calm.

Ruby lived until 1967. Jackie Kennedy died May 1994 aged 64. President Johnson died January 1994, aged 64 also.

Without doubt at the age of 12, these sequences of events were the most drama laden, disturbing, unprecedented happenings I had ever experienced. Not just kids such as me, but billions of adults the world over remained shocked by the occurrences that took place right there before us in those few days in November 1963.

The only time anything would ever come near to this again would be on 11th September 2001.

Chapter Six
I Saw Her Standing There (1964-1965)

"Here you are Jack, here's a quid for you". It was June 1964, and my dad had just passed to me a crisp £1 note which I looked at, admired briefly, then placed carefully away in my khaki shorts pocket.

I thought to myself, "How come he's only given me a quid? That was just his stake money. He would never have won £32 without those tips I gave him."

Santa Claus ridden by Scobie Breasley had a few days earlier won the Epsom Derby. Two days later Homeward Bound with Greville Starkey on board had won the Oaks. My dad had a £1 double which returned over £32. That was a week's wage to him in 1964.

I had given him the tips a week before when he had asked me who I fancied for the two races. I had no hesitation in giving him the names of the eventual winners. I had of course been following flat racing for three years by the time of the 1964 Epsom meeting.

Little did my dad know, but I did not choose those horses. Maurice Woodruff did. Maurice was quite a famous psychic at the time and in the T.V. Times of Christmas 1963, he had made certain predictions for the coming year, 1964. Amongst his forecasts, many of which I had rapidly overlooked, were his predictions for the Derby and Oaks winners. For the Derby, he had suggested a horse with a name that brings seasonal joy to children. For the Oaks, a horse whose name suggests a happy occasion.

It wasn't the first time he had done this. In the 1962 edition of the Christmas TV Times he had forecast in his own way the winners of the 1963 Derby and Oaks. I had remembered that, and eagerly awaited the 1963 edition of the magazine. So, I never told my dad the secret. I simply allowed him to go around telling people that his son was a top tipster, and would probably be the new Templegate in years to come.

It just makes me think that there are definitely people out there who can see the future. Apparently, the actor Peter Sellers relied greatly upon Maurice Woodruff and would never make a major career or life decision without consulting him first. I wonder if Maurice ever backed horses himself? With that ability I certainly would have.

The year 1964 was akin to a butterfly emerging from its chrysalis. The old rock'n'roll songs were still being pounded out by bands in Sheffield. The Memorial Hall in Hillsborough had old rock'n'roll type groups banging out live stuff two or three times a week. This was okay for the 17 plus crowd, but amongst the younger element we had found a taste for something new.

The Beatles had forged a path for new sounds in the Kinks, the Animals, the Zombies, and last but not least the Rolling Stones, However, even more rebellious and more provocative were the Pretty Things. Lead singer Phil May claimed he had the longest male hair in the UK. He probably had. They also claimed that adults hated them more than the Stones. They probably did.

The Beatles were easy on the eye for the young kids' parents. They wore suits, laughed, joked, fooled around, and were good at writing sing along music with rock'n'roll beats. The Stones, Pretty Things, Kinks etc. were different. Primarily they were different because they were geographically different. Their hair was longer too.

England is tribal, and the raw Anglo Saxon sounds of the South East contrasted with the Liverpudlian Irish/Lancashire sounds of the Merseyside movement.

Great singles were beginning to be released. "House of the Rising Sun"; "You Really Got Me"; "Not Fade Away"; "She's Not There". The Beatles hit back with "Can't Buy Me Love".

During these exciting times, aged just 12, I saw the Rolling Stones live at Sheffield City Hall. I went with some friends from school. I couldn't hear the music. There was too much screaming going on. Apparently their setlist included "Come On"; "Route 66"; "Carol"; "Walking the Dog"; "Not Fade Away". It didn't matter what they sang. Just to watch them was a revelation. I couldn't hear properly afterwards for two weeks.

Then it happened. I saw Sandie Shaw on Ready Steady Go one Friday teatime and my body was tingling with a feeling I had not experienced before. "Always something there to remind me", she sang. I was mesmerised. What a beguiling beauty. She was 17, and I was 12-and-a-half. It didn't matter. She would one day be mine. It never happened.

Sandie, a working-class girl from Dagenham had stolen my heart. I think working class was the key to her charm. She had one of those lovely English faces. Not stunningly beautiful, but Anglo Saxon pretty. Incredibly pretty. Legs to match someone once said. I wouldn't argue. So, by the time I was 12-and-a-half, I had cavorted with Juliet Prowse, Ursula Andress, Marilyn Monroe, and now Sandie Shaw. In my mind's eye only of course.

When would it stop? An experience that year told me it must never stop, ever. On a dark night in 1964 I was alone looking in to the window of Thomas electrical and record shop on Middlewood Road. I felt safe and warm in my own environment. That is until I felt a hand on my shoulder. I looked around and a man aged maybe early twenties said quietly "do you want to come around the back of this shop for some fun?" Well I knew it was too dark for ludo or tiddledywinks so I pulled away from him, took a couple of backwards steps, then ran the 50 yards home in a very fast time. I barged through the back door and stood panting heavily.

"What's up Jack?" asked my mum and dad almost in unison.

"It's this man", I spluttered

"Which man?" they asked

"He asked me to go behind Thomas shop".

"You didn't, did you?"

"No, no, no".

"I'll kill him", shouted my dad. "Come with me. See if you can spot him" We rushed out together. I'd never seen my dad's face like that since he'd threatened to hit me for fighting my cousin Malcolm after he had tried to nick my bag of black grapes. Anyway, we didn't see the guilty party. Good job too. Seriously, my dad would have killed him.

So, that in a nutshell is why I remain committed firmly to the fairer sex.

The Great Train Robbers got sentenced to a total of 307 years' imprisonment in 1964. Harsh justice I feel. Just because the establishment had been shaken to its core by this gang, they were sentenced heavily as a deterrent to others who may have planned something similar. Just my opinion of course.

Also in deep trouble in 1964 was Nelson Mandela who was jailed for life for sabotage. We wouldn't get to see him again for a while. It wasn't a good year for criminals. In February, former jailbird Sonny Liston was well beaten in the ring, against all odds, by Cassius Clay. Nobody in their right minds thought this was going to happen, but Clay proving he could take punches as well as land them won by technical knockout before the start of round seven.

My first year at King Edward VII school ended in July 1964 and I was mightily relieved to have six full weeks of freedom away from the homework, discipline, Victorian values and plethora of middle class twits.

We went on holiday to a caravan park in Fleetwood, Lancashire. To be honest I don't remember too much about it apart from the fact that there was a gas storage tank overlooking the site. I do recall swimming in a freezing cold outdoor pool on the seafront, and demonstrating my new array of aquatic talents to my parents. Other than that I remember thinking that I would have preferred the Norfolk Broads, or Great Yarmouth. Anyway, I wasn't at school. That was the main thing.

According to me I should have been born in 1965. This was the year of the snake in the Chinese zodiac. Personality traits for the year of the snake indicate individuals who are intelligent, wise, materialistic, courageous. According to my grandad (Watson), my hair was far too long, and I needed a man's haircut. Not only that, but "all you young uns have got your brains in your bollocks". I guess he was right, and I dare not argue with him. So, as my hair grew I avoided him. As my bollocks grew I kept them in check.

1965 was a big year, not only for me, but for the world. This was the year that Sir Winston Churchill died. I remember watching the funeral on television. I think it was on a Saturday morning in January, and for some reason we had the curtains drawn. With the passing of Churchill, sad as it was, it was almost as if a release button had been pressed to take our whole generation a little more in to the future. The last hero, the last icon from Victoriana, the last great leader had left our world, and suddenly we began to live life in technicolour.

Later in July, as a complete contrast, Ronnie Biggs, one of the train robbers escaped from Wandsworth prison. He was free for nearly 40 years before he returned voluntarily to Britain from Brazil.

In May 1965, Mohammed Ali (formerly Cassius Clay) knocked out Sonny Liston in round one to prove once and for all that his 1964 victory was not a fluke. He never stopped talking after that.

"Think of all the hate there is in Red China, then look around to Selma Alabama. You may leave here for four days in space, but when you return it's the same old place."

Recorded in 1965, the "Eve of Destruction" song contained the above words. The song, all way through was extremely powerful. Recorded by Barry McGuire, if released today, many of its lyrics would still be relevant. This was the era of the protest song. Bob Dylan, Donovan, Buffy Saint-Marie, Country Joe and the Fish, Joan Baez, all wrote and recorded music that aired their views on politics, war, racism, freedom. The escalation of the war in Vietnam added fuel to the fire. The world was changing rapidly, and young people in free countries worldwide were making their views known through all forms of media. People in the Far East still were immolating themselves often daily. No, I'm not going through that one again.

Away from the protest scene, in fact as far away as you could get, the Beatles were making "Help", the film and the album. Despite my stance about, "I'm no Beatles fan, give me the Stones any day", I loved "Help". I bought the album and thought every track fantastic, particularly the title track, and "The Night Before". The film was hilarious, and remains very high on my funniest films ever list. It's not quite on the level of Life of Brian, or Airplane, but it certainly gives Paleface, and the Lemondrop Kid, a run for their money.

I watched Help in the Gaumont Cinema with my cousin John. He was wearing a cap because he had been ordered to the barber shop by his dad. He had been given a neat short back and sides, and if not for the cap would have been ridiculed for having the shortest hair in the cinema.

Help, in my opinion was the best film of 1965. It didn't have much opposition. The big films of the year were Sound of Music; Doctor Zhivago; Cincinnati Kid; Goldfinger; Thunderball. Only the two Bond films were of interest to me. I had sneaked in to the Kinema to watch them both. Great use of the back door theory. Neither could compare to Doctor No, or From Russia with Love. Only the gorgeous Shirley Eaton, stripped almost naked, and painted gold lives as a lasting memory from Goldfinger.

Around that time I had a girlfriend for a couple of weeks. She was tall, blonde, slim, blue eyed and named Diana. My old friend Lesley had introduced me to her, and we got along well. I had never at that point met anyone so good looking before in the flesh. We walked and held hands, and I was proud to be with her. She had the looks of Shirley Eaton, but without gold paint. We went to the Kinema a couple of times, snogged, told jokes, walked in the park, and that was about it. I saw her maybe 10 years later and she was driving a Mercedes. I was still using the bus.

March to September brought us the speedway season. In 1965 and 1966 we must have gone to every home meeting. To be honest the sport itself wasn't particularly interesting. The Sheffield Tigers had their home fixtures every Thursday. I think we paid one shilling and nine pence entrance fee. More expensive to enter than the Kinema, it at least allowed you to see girls in relative daylight and in August as the days shortened under floodlight. Sheffield speedway was a great meeting place for our age group at that time. In fact instead of watching the racing, groups would simply have a walk around the stadium eyeing up the opposite sex. The music was good too. Between races, from the tannoy we could hear great stuff such as "Satisfaction"; "Baby Please Don't Go"; "Watcha Gonna do about it"; "I can't Explain"; and more.

One clear, starry night in early September I met my future wife there. Cousin John and me were on our fourth or fifth circuit of the stadium, and just passing the third bend. John was waving at two girls who were standing about 10 rows of steps from the bottom wall. The lights from the "dog club bar" shone out upon them.

"Who's that? " I asked.

"Christine and Colleen. They're cousins. I go to school with them."

"That small one is beautiful," I drawled.

We walked up the steps towards them. Reaching them I looked Christine straight in the eye. She only had one. It was right in the middle of her forehead. (sorry my love, but I couldn't resist the Les Dawson type joke). Anyway, she was truly gorgeous. I just stared at her. She had grey eyes that sparkled, a lovely skin, light brown hair and wore a blue and white polka dot dress. I wanted to see more of her. On our way home I instructed my cousin John to find Christine at school the very next day, and ask that she meet me for a date.

The answer came back next day "No".

"John, did you say no?"

"Yes, no."

"Do you mean yes or no?"

"I mean no."

I didn't like people saying no to me, especially when I wanted them to say yes. She was in my mind, and I couldn't escape her. So, I kept asking John to ask her, and I kept getting the knock back.

Then a few weeks later, Owlerton fair. Christine was an Owlerton girl, and lived just 100 yards from the fairground. She was there with her mother and younger sister, I spotted her and smiled. She smiled back "I'm in here", I thought.

I walked over, and just as her little sister was about to hook a duck I said, "I'll walk you home." It was turning dark. She looked at her mother and said, "If you want to go home now, Jack will walk me up the road." Her mother grabbed hold of Gillian's hand and saying goodbye set off on her way back home. We were alone together, all but for the noise of the fairground, and "Mr Tambourine Man" by the Byrds blasting out loudly from the waltzer.

We walked around for a while, exchanging conversation about the usual teenage things.

"I'd better go back home now to help my mum," she said.

As we left the fair, and the noise behind us began to fade, I reached for Christine's hand, and after a little resistance began to hold it nearer to me. Reaching the yard where her home was, we stopped, turned to each other, and kissed. It was a true magic moment.

We didn't make another date. We simply smiled at each other, and said goodnight.

Chapter Seven
God Only Knows (1966)

"You cannot have this girlfriend any longer."
Mr "Flink" Jackstone, deputy headmaster of King Edward VII school was a small, wiry man with the slow smile of Jack Nicholson.

I bit my lip and tried to remain respectful.

"Your attention to this girl is interfering with your schoolwork, and it cannot continue."

"Sir, I'm not going to give the girl up," I answered.

Flink looked at me with angry eyes. "Then Watson, I have a choice for you. You either stop seeing her or you will no longer be selected for the school football and cricket teams that represent us so well."

"Sir, I am not going to stop seeing her."

"So be it then Watson. You have made your choice. I will inform the masters responsible for team selection that you are no longer to be picked to play. You may go."

I made my exit from his office without a word. I resisted the temptation to slam the door behind me, but I was furious. What right did they have to pry in to my life? They were employed to educate me, not to robotise me.

Incidents like this made me hate the system more. Not just the school system, but the whole system. The system we were expected to conform to and to be part of, the system that insisted that you cut your hair. The system that for centuries had transformed our working-class boys in to soldiers who were then turned in to machines of slaughter and machines of rape and plunder all over the globe. These were my views at the time I hasten to add. My views in this day and age are somewhat different.

"Well, they can just stick it", I thought, "and I'll go scrubbing decks, somewhere warm, and take Christine with me."

If their action in stopping me playing sport was intended to hurt me then they failed. I would miss the football and cricket I had been involved with for three years plus, but I would miss Christine more. I loved her. I did not love the school.

Summer 1966, and before I had got back to seeing Christine regularly, I was alone in our family maisonette on Liberty Hill playing Subbuteo in a game of me versus me, I had my trusty Bush transistor radio beside me. I was tuned in to Radio 270, a pirate station moored in international waters off the North Yorkshire coast near Scarborough.

Suddenly without introduction I heard the most beautiful song, "I may not always love you, as long as there are stars above you". It was of course "God Only Knows" by the Beach Boys. Its simple, profound lyrics and beautiful harmonies stopped me in my tracks. It was a spiritual moment. I immediately loved the song, and still do now, just as much as ever.

Radio 270 operated for around 15 months, but it was fantastic. Miles away in Sheffield we could pick up the transmission without interference, and the jockeys played good music the whole day through. Of course, 1966 was a very good year for music, and this made life easier for them to play those excellent sounds.

"Summer in the City"; "Good Vibrations"; "For What It's Worth"; "Paint It Black"; "Monday Monday"; "Substitute". All fantastic, ground-breaking tracks, each and every one.

Hillsborough (courtesy of Harry Ainscough and www.copperbeechstudios.co.uk)

The summer weather was dreadful however, but around kids of our age a new world of optimism was about to start. Works by the Beach Boys with album "Pet Sounds", and "Revolver" by the Beatles were opening up a panorama of future sounding experimental sounds. Our generation suddenly found itself "different" to anything that had gone before.

In Britain, if not America, it was a time of optimism. At the height of the summer England had won the World Cup, and the news was full of it for weeks. I had watched the match at home that Saturday afternoon, and witnessed my father's few tears of emotion as England lifted the trophy. I never saw him cry before that moment, and I never saw him cry again after. That doesn't mean to say he was a tough, bitter, unthinking sort. Far from it. He probably reserved his tears for more private moments.

I was still feeling the pain of my football team Sheffield Wednesday losing the FA Cup final that year. It really did mean more to me than England winning, and every time someone mentions 1966 now, I immediately think of that warm May Day at Wembley when, after leading 2-0 well in to the second half, Everton came back strongly to beat us 3-2.

I was there at Wembley that day with my half cousin Peter. I had managed to get a ticket for face value cost of 10 shillings just two days before the final. A lad at school lived next door to Wednesday chairman Eric Taylor, and he sorted it out for me. Can you imagine nowadays allowing two lads aged 14 out of your sight for 18 hours to travel to London and back by coach knowing that they were to stand in a vast crowd of 100,000 that would roar and sway for two whole hours like a relentless giant tide washing against the shore? It just wouldn't happen now. Risk assessment? Didn't exist then.

The day after the final, Sunday, I saw Christine at Hillsborough Corner. She was with her cousin Sylvia. She had a few spots and told me that she was just recovering from chicken pox.

Hundreds of people were standing at the corner. They were all waiting for the open top bus carrying the returning Wednesday team from Wembley. They didn't have a trophy to show, but deserved the applause and cheers they were about to receive.

I hadn't seen Christine since January when she had been hobbling around on crutches after having had an operation for osteomyelitis of the knee. After our first "date" in the previous September we had seen each other a few times, but had never gone out together regularly. We were after all both only 14. We hadn't fallen out with each other. I had moved to Liberty Hill, Stannington and we were a bus ride and more apart now.

I still thought she was gorgeous, but we weren't destined to meet again for a further 3 months or so.

Another girl came in to my life. Intensely bored by the day, I was looking through the window of our maisonette towards the site of the new pub that was being built over the road. Being two floors up, I had a great observation point, and could see all around, straight across, to the left, and to the right.

She appeared from the right, walking towards the bus stop below our window. She cruised like a model, parading herself with ceremony. I hadn't seen her before. We had been on the estate for six months, and I had never caught sight of her at all. As she drew nearer I could see the lovely, wavy black hair, shoulder length, bouncing around her shoulders. Well-formed for her age, she knew it and knew just how to show it.

I shouted downwards on to the street, "Hello, what's your name?"

She looked up. "I'm Linda, and you are Jack aren't you?"

"Yes I am. Wait just there. I'll be with you in a minute".

As I walked up to her she was nervously messing with a bracelet on her wrist.

"Where are you off to?" I asked.

"I'm just off to my friend's house."

"Well what if you don't bother, and just take a walk with me?"

She nodded her head in approval. We walked off down Fairbarn Road in the general direction of Rivelin Valley.

Linda was a lovely looking girl, and knew it. Ten years later we all saw Lynda Carter as Wonder Woman. This young Linda could have been a junior version in 1966. Without the costume of course. Well, not exactly without the costume, but wearing something else instead. Obviously!

We saw each other most nights for six or seven weeks. We got on really well. The Rivelin Valley was right on our doorstep, and we spent most summer nights there strolling the paths by the river. I got to meet Linda's younger brother and sister, and sometimes we stayed in their house on Liberty Place when it was quiet, and nobody around.

Sadly, for some reason I began to get a bit bored with it all. Not with Linda, but the repetition of doing the same thing night after night. At that age though there was little on offer to entertain kids growing up other than television and street corners. We drifted apart, but remained friends. She was a special girl.

For a change, one afternoon I met up with a friend from school, Mario. R. We decided to meet in town, and try to get in the ABC cinema to watch

Plague of the Zombies. The film was rated X, and we got in despite being short of 16 by a year or so. The ABC had only been in operation for three or four years and its interior was modern, sumptuous and grand compared to the run down old cinemas dotted liberally around the streets of Sheffield.

It was an afternoon screening of the film, and the auditorium must have been 90% empty. We had the choice of several hundred seats, and opted to sit about 10 rows back from the screen with hardly anyone to the front or either side of us.

The film started and with nervous anticipation we awaited the first real action. Well, we soon got it. Action that is, but not on the screen. Two oriental gentlemen came and sat beside us. One at my left, and one at Mario's right. Now, considering there were probably a further 800 seats for them to choose from, I found it rather strange. As my dear dad once commented on a very poorly attended Hillsborough football match when someone sat right next to him, "If I went to live on The Sea of Tranquillity some dick would come and live beside me."

The oriental gentlemen were shuffling in their seats and smiling. I nudged Mario, and motioned to get up and move seats. After all we had plenty of choice. We walked a further 20 or so rows back, and hoping that Charlie Chan and his mate wouldn't follow, settled down again to watch the film.

They did move though, and followed us again, just as we thought we might have lost them.

"Christ's sake Mario, let's go again, "I sighed. We did, and finished up about 5 rows from the back. A bit darker there, we thought we might at last be safe. Not to be. The insurgents arrived again, and as they were attempting to settle beside us Mario shouted "Just run Jack. Jack, run". Bit like Forrest Gump I guess.

We clambered over the last few rows and spotting an exit sign made our way down a few flights of steps and in to the bright sunshine outside. So, presuming these guys had motives of a sexual nature, I had escaped for a second time. They may have been innocent and just wanted us to be extras in a re-make of Inn of the Sixth Happiness. No, I think it was the long hair. It puzzled me. What was their motivation? What did they achieve by trying to mess with young adolescent males? Worst of all, with the streets full of beautiful young mini-skirted girls on the loose, why should they really need to mess with boys? I knew which side my bread was buttered, if you pardon the expression. I didn't understand them, and I don't even now.

So, Plague of the Zombies. We never got to see that. All the other decent films made during that year were also A or X rated. Our Man Flint; Alfie;

The Good, the Bad and the Ugly; Cathy Come Home;

The Batman film was released however. The film was actually named Batman The Movie and starred Adam West and Burt Ward, the same two who played Batman and Robin in the TV series, also aired for the first time in 1966.

Right at the end of that summer, and just short of my fifteenth birthday a group of us were standing outside around Chinny's fish and chip shop on Holme Lane Hillsborough. A warm night but dark at 9pm, the lights from the shop glared brightly on to our small gathering. I felt a tug on my shirt. I turned to see a little girl of about nine looking up at me. It was Christine's sister Gillian.

"Jack, will you go out with my sister Christine?" she asked with those sweet baby blue eyes blinking away against the light.

"Where is she?" I asked

"She's over there", she replied pointing at Christine who was 20 yards away.

Christine looked as good as ever. Her shyness at that moment only added to her appeal.

"Tell her "yes".

"So, you'll go out with her again then?"

"Yes, I will. I think she's beautiful."

Gillian skipped away to Christine, and they joined hands before waving to me and heading on their way home.

That moment was the key to the rest of my life.

Chapter Eight
Purple Haze / Liberty

The westerly winds come in off the Atlantic, bear down on Lancashire, climb up and over the Pennines, then sweep on to the western edges of the city of Sheffield. The Stannington area unprotected from this force, bears the brunt of this.

In November 1965 we moved to the new council estate in Stannington. For years I had lived in the relatively warmer, sheltered area of Hillsborough. This transition came as an almighty shock. It was cold, bleak, and unwelcoming. Already at the end of November, the snow was mounting. Snow fell as I'd never seen it fall before. It didn't come straight down or even come in at an angle. It sort of milled around randomly just like in a glass snow globe, then deposited itself menacingly inch upon inch. Just two miles from Proctor Place, it felt like another world.

The place we now lived in was a two bedroom maisonette on Liberty Hill. These were built in blocks of 12 homes. six dwellings on the ground floor, and six on the floors above. We had a bathroom, running hot water, and a form of central heating that was quite basic, but effective. So at least we could keep warm, and keep clean.

The day after we moved in the snow had stopped falling, and a weak, watery sun emerged to greet us around 9am. Being on the upper floor enabled us to see for miles around, literally. Our view encompassed the Rivelin Valley, Crosspool, Den Bank, Crookes, Bole Hills, Walkley. Quite a spectacular view, and one that I never would have believed could have been possible the day before.

Looking from the window to the left, and we could see one of the three tower blocks that had been erected on the estate. They were each 14 floors high and I used to wonder to myself just how far one could see from their vantage point. I found it for myself some years later. You could see to Rotherham and beyond, probably 15 miles and more on a clear day.

The estate was still being finished when we moved there. All the roads except the main road through to Stannington village were bogged down with mud. No cars came through. They would never have got back to the main road.

I got to school by catching the number 7 bus on the main road all the way through to the city centre. Then another bus took me onwards to King Edward VII school. My mother and younger brother Alan, just five-years-old, walked to Shooters Grove School through the weather and mud day after day. It was almost like being thrown out to live on the edge of The Arctic Circle. I hated those first six months.

Then came Spring 1966, and things began to look better. The sun shone and it poured its light over everywhere we looked. From the window, we could see even further, and all felt good. About this time, I spotted Linda for the first time, and we got on well.

I got a job delivering newspapers which earned me 30 shillings a week. This was more money than I'd ever had, and I felt like a wealthy young, well to do prince.

For the first time in six months I began to see people, and recognise them. Up until this point everyone from the estate had hid under hats, scarves, big coats, balaclavas, and nobody was recognisable from one day to the next. Just like us, most people had arrived on the estate a few months earlier from low lying slum-ridden districts, and they too were not used to this harsh weather.

Delivering the papers enabled me to get in conversation with people from the neighbourhood, and to make friends and acquaintances. I quickly learned that on the whole estate only one other lad attended the same school as me, and he was two years younger. Almost everyone attended Myers Grove School. Linda still went to Wisewood School as that was the area that she hailed from.

Just about everybody seemed to get on well. It was quite a welcoming, close knit community. People had been thrown together from all four corners of the city, and seemed to be enjoying their new lives on the windswept hills that housed us.

In that same spring/summer of 1966 a new pub that was to be named Charles Turnbull was being built directly across from our maisonette. The other side of our estate, Deer Park, already had its own pub, The Deerstalker, and whenever I passed it on the bus, it always seemed lively, bright and busy.

Ten minute's walk downhill from our home and through the woods from Liberty Hill, and you were in the fabulous Rivelin Valley. "Rivs" was, and still is, a true wonderland for children and adults alike. The river that gives its name to the valley runs through the area, deep in parts, but mostly shallow. It joins with the river Loxley at Malin Bridge. Both rivers are alive with trout, and on bright days during all four seasons the fish can be seen gliding and turning quickly amongst the rocks on the river bed. You walk on the pathways through the valley and although you are in the city of Sheffield and in postal district S6, you could almost be in a national park in New Zealand for instance.

All this on our doorstep just a few minute's walk from Liberty Hill. As the summer of 1966 came and went, and autumn turned to winter, I counted my blessings and was grateful that I now lived in a brand new home with my fantastic family, and was reconciled with the gorgeous Christine. The only dark cloud that surrounded me was the school I attended. Archaic, Victorian, almost a dark satanic mill but without the industry involved there, King Edward VII school imprisoned me day on day, but would never get to institutionalise me or steal my soul, as it did with many others.

We had some great characters with great nicknames on the estate. The list included, Shandygaff; Delilah; Miss World; Moon River; Blue Suede Shoes; Twiggy; Outer Limits; Nut Nut; Puffballs; Lizzie Hut; Zoony. My favourite though was dear old Purple Diarrhoea. He came and sat beside me on a bus journey from Liberty Hill to Hillsborough Corner on a pleasant evening in early Summer 1968. The conversation went something like this...

"Hello Jack, I'm alright to sit next to you aren't I?"

"Yes. I don't see why not."

"Well Jack you see I've got a problem."

"Oh. Is it school or a girl or something like that?"

"Oh no Jack, it's much more serious. I've been ill these last few days. I've had diarrhoea. Not just ordinary diarrhoea. Oh no. It was purple diarrhoea."

"Is that catching?"

"I don't think so. My mum and dad are alright."

At this point I looked around tentatively to see if anyone was listening in. There were some nice girls on the bus dressed well, and making their way to town for a night out. I smiled politely at them.

"You've not got it now have you?"

"Well I never know when it might strike Jack. I've ruined six pairs of pants and two pairs of Levi Sta Prest this week alone."

"If you feel it coming on between here and Hillsborough Corner will you move and let me go downstairs ?"

"Of course I will Jack. Are those jeans Lee Rider?"

"Yes, brand new and this white denim jacket is Wrangler, so don't bleedin start with it."

He nodded in agreement, and assumed a silent mode. The bus pulled in to the stop before Hillsborough Corner. He looked at me and grimaced. I wondered what was happening. He farted loudly and in three seconds flat, I escaped my seat, manoeuvred my way around him and got to the foot of the bus stairs, all the time praying for the next stop. The bus got to Hillsborough Corner, and I jumped off as soon as the doors opened. Christine was there waiting for me.

"What's up with you?" She asked "you look petrified".

"You'd never believe it", came my reply.

I explained in full and she kept three feet away from me all night despite my protests.

He did recover. I saw him a few weeks later, and before I could ask he blurted out, "I'm alright Jack. I feel much better."

"Good. I'm in a rush. See you soon."

That's where the legend of Purple Diarrhoea began.

The Charles Turnbull pub had opened and was an immediate hit with the locals. Of course, I was too young to go in there as were many of my contemporaries. In those days, you just didn't go in a pub if you were not of age. There was a genuine fear that police would walk in and do you for underage drinking. My first pint was on the other side of the estate in the Deerstalker. I was 17 and the pint cost one shilling and elevenpence, roughly equivalent to nine-and-a-half-pence nowadays. I remember staring at the door just in case the police burst in, threw me to the floor, kicked me in the ribs, let their dogs savage me and then threw me down the cold steps inside West Bar police station. I needn't have worried. They must have thought I was small fry. In fact I was.

My dad went across to the Turnbull once or twice a week and joined the darts team. They were quite good by all accounts. When he wasn't in there he would come to our door to let me in at the usual time of 10.35pm. He would greet me with, "Jack, just nip across to the Turnbull for me and get me 20 Park Drive and a Crunchie". Despite my objections I always did as he bid and the off sales in the pub would welcome me in there three or four times a week.

It was really quite a favoured existence on Liberty Hill. With the roads all finished, and the pub completed, a small row of shops sprung up and soon we were all living in a sort of modern utopia well away from the grime, smoke and pollutant chemicals that had followed us everywhere during our Sheffield childhood. Of course these pollutants earned the working class their money in our city, and the early morning buses from the estate were packed with men wearing flat caps and sweat towels as they and their forebears had for years. Looking eastwards from our fantastic window view you could see across the city where giant chimneys belched out vast plumes of smoke in to the sky. The prevailing westerlies made sure that these dangerous gases and chemicals were pushed out towards Rotherham and beyond and did not touch our new found kingdom on the hillside.

It was a special time in a special place. Liberty by name, Liberty by nature. The second half of the sixties saw vast changes in not only our society, but also in our mentality, our senses and our approach to life. Not just for our generation did this happen but also for our parents who seemed to share an enlightenment themselves.

At the age of 18 I had to leave Liberty Hill. My circumstances dictated this. I still hold a yearning for the place now, and indeed always will do.

Chapter Nine
Night Of Fear (1967)

If you thought the summer of love was a pleasant, smiley, sun-filled time of laughter, friendliness and sweet delight, think again. As the hippies and pseudo hippies gathered in San Francisco, and the West Coast scene chugged its way through acres of cannabis, the Eastern States became a virtual battleground. Throughout June, July and August the cities of Buffalo (N.Y); Newark (N,J); Plainfield (N,J); Jay(FLA); Minneapolis(MN); Milwaukee(WI); Washington (DC) were all subject to rioting, looting, stand off and hate.

In Detroit there were 43 dead, 7000 arrested, 1,300 buildings destroyed, and 2,700 businesses looted.

Newark had six days of rioting and looting leaving 26 dead, 727 injured, 1,500 arrested with an estimated $10 million worth of damage.

The cause of the riots was simply the African American population feeling disenfranchised. The populace had little or no faith in the legal system, and took out their frustrations on the police and local community.

So, just as the whole country was descending in to a maelstrom of drugs, guns, fire and murder, it's movie moguls released three of its best films for several years.

In August, Bonnie and Clyde, and In the Heat of The Night were released. A little after the strangest summer in decades came Cool Hand Luke.

God bless America. God bless your writers, your actors, your producers, your directors. I went to see all three movies not long after their release in the UK. I had Christine with me of course, and I believe we saw all three films at the Esseldo Cinema, Southey Green.

These movies all had a similar theme running through the storyline. Stories from The South containing desperation and fear.

The magnificent Bonnie and Clyde. A story about two young Texans who, along with their gang, left a trail of death and misery as they traversed the states of Texas, Arkansas, Indiana, Missouri, Iowa and Indiana. Eventually they met their inevitable end in the woodlands of Louisiana, just when they thought they might be safe.

Warren Beatty and Faye Dunaway played the renegade duo. How superb they looked, and how well they posed and wore their clothes. Probably the best-looking male and female duo ever in movies. The image they portrayed still looks fantastic 50 years later. I didn't want them to die in that movie. Nobody in the cinema did. The deaths were horrific but filmed so well. I still read now whatever I can about the young Texans. They lived their lives during the Great Depression, and nobody, just as happens now, does any favours for the working classes. They had to step out and do themselves favours. Love for each other carried them through until Louisiana. Bonnie and Clyde, my second favourite film ever.

Cool Hand Luke, starring Paul Newman and set in Florida, along with In the Heat of The Night, starring Rod Steiger and Sidney Poitier and set in Mississippi, make up this excellent trio of Southern-based films. All three had a big influence on me as an adolescent. They gave me an interest in all things Southern from Levis to Coca Cola to Robert E. Lee.

These influences have pretty much stayed with me. I love the clothes of Bonnie and Clyde. I love the attitude of Cool Hand Luke. I love the grit and atmosphere of In the Heat of The Night.

A year later I took my history in G.C.E "O" level on two subjects. The first was British History 1901-1951. The second was the American Civil War. I passed easily on both. It was almost as if I had lived those two eras. I found it so easy.

By this uncertain summer of 1967 I had been going out with Christine for almost one year. As young as we were, we were very close. I was intensely jealous, and watched her every movement.

She was so lovely. So, so pretty and petite. I couldn't get enough of her. She was buying clothes that looked good on her. Neither of us were really influenced by the hippy scene of that year. Christine had saved her money and bought a three-quarter length dark green leather coat. Real leather too. You could smell the quality. She followed this by buying a beige coloured suede coat. Again, full in length, and cut in such a way that the shape of it fitted tightly on her. Never one for trousers or jeans in those days, she mostly wore dresses, colourful and fitted. She always looked smart.

I was so proud of her, and seeing her as she was, I was just really pleased that the small-minded staff of King Edward VII School had given me their alternative about playing sport or choosing Christine. The choice was never a contest. Only ever one winner. She was always the winner.

In November that year I bought two tickets for a concert at Sheffield City

Hall. The concert was a tour of the UK and Jimi Hendrix was top of the bill. Also on the bill were Amen Corner, The Move, Pink Floyd, and The Nice. All this for five shillings per ticket (equivalent to 25p today). Amazing value, and great memories.

We were seated about six rows from the back, downstairs, and so didn't have the best view. Now this type of music wasn't exactly Christine's cup of tea, but she seemed ok with Amen Corner and The Move. Both groups performed more "pop type" songs which suited her taste. The Pink Floyd performance with lights and alien instrumentals had her shaking her head in disbelief. Of course, The Nice finishing their set with "America", saw her with fingers in ears. Then the man himself entered from the right and the City Hall erupted. All year I had been listening to Hendrix, and I felt his songs and guitar were a complete change of direction, and breath of fresh air on the scene. Jimi contorted, gyrated, twisted and smashed his way through the set. The playlist was 'Stone Free'; 'Hey Joe'; 'Purple Haze'; 'Foxy Lady'; 'The Wind Cries Mary' and 'Wild Thing'.

My God, five shillings for all that. What a gift. What a sight. What a memory. As the hall emptied and everyone poured out in to the dark, wet November Sheffield streets, I asked Christine what she made of it. "I didn't understand it. My ears hurt, and it frightened me", came her reply. Ah, bless her. What she had witnessed was not to be messed with I thought to myself. Here was the greatest guitar player in the world. We had watched his short set that night in awe, many of us. In my opinion, even now, the greatest blues/rock guitarist ever. I have never seen or heard better. Sadly, he had so much more to offer. Like many others from that era, his untimely death took away forever the chance to judge him further.

The year itself was a mess. Not particularly for me, but the world. Whenever we see old footage of hippies dancing and swirling like saplings in a storm, or handing out flowers to unsuspecting passers-by, we must realise one thing. The world was in chaos. The whole hippie scene was a diversion from the truth.

The Cold War was getting colder. The six-day war between Israel and her Arab neighbours flared up, then died down (temporarily). China exploded her first hydrogen bomb, thereby giving yet another country the power to kill millions with just one press of a button.

In San Francisco 10,000 marched in protest against the Vietnam War. To no avail however. By the end of 1967 a staggering total of 474,300 U.S. soldiers were deployed in Vietnam. Unthinkable. The best part of half a million young men sent out to a foreign outpost simply to stop the spread of communism. An enormous waste of young lives. As somebody said at the time, "when will we ever learn, when will we ever learn?"

Meanwhile, back in King Edward VII School, Sheffield, I was behaving like a complete twat. My friends Plong, Rosie, and our D'artagnan like accomplice Richard.M, had been attracting trouble like a magnet since the back end of 1966. We built a reputation throughout the school, and of course with a reputation, especially a bad one, trouble, often quite serious, follows.

The four of us collected in a 12 month period, 106 strokes of the cane. I only had 19 of those, so I was quite a little angel by comparison. My offences were smoking, spitting, swearing and verbal abuse of a teacher. The cane was applied to our rear end, and in hindsight was very, very distasteful. If you were caught perpetrating such serious offences as I was then you had to follow procedure.

"Watson, fetch the cane," would be the order. So, you had to troop off to the staff room, knock on the door, give your name, form, and the name of the teacher who had sent you. The cane was then handed to you along with a document that had to be filled in by the flagellist.

"Wait in the corridor Watson", you would be told as you returned to the scene of your offence and handed over the cane.

So you waited, all the time putting on your best Marlon Brando face in an act of defiance. The teacher would then re-appear with another teacher who would act as witness.

"I'm going to give you four strokes Watson. Be prepared."

"Prepared?" I thought. "How the hell can you prepare for this. At least Billy Bunter used to get some warning of these beatings, and could stuff some exercise books down his pants."

"Lift your jacket and bend right over Watson."

"Something wrong about all this. I'm going to tell my dad," I pondered as the first stroke connected.

"Bastard." I hissed between my teeth.

Then the second landed, and then the third catching me high around my right hip.

"Horrible, horrible twat," I wanted to shout. Finally the fourth stroke, biting hard in to the exact area where the first had landed.

"Return to your desk Watson," came the order. I raised myself up slowly, and looked the teacher in the eye. He searched my face for tears. There were no tears. I looked back threateningly at him and wanted to say, "you'll have to hit me harder than that. I was brought up in Hillsborough, not some leafy avenue in Sheffield 11."

I hated the staff and the school. Since I had been forced to give up playing sport for the school I detested every moment. The only thing I enjoyed was being with my partners in crime, Plong, Rosie, and Richard.M. Good lads, all of them.

The four of us took a mass flogging one day. It was after an "O" level exam in the summer of 1967. We walked down to our usual position at the bottom of the school grounds for a well-earned recreational fag after a particularly hard exam inside the cramped school gym. We all lit up, and relaxed, backs against the stone wall. Not for long though. Halfway down our Players' No. 6, PE teacher Mr. Harbistone appeared. He said nothing for a few seconds. He just stared at us. We knew what we were in for, and threw the cigarettes to the ground, and stamped on them. Plong however did not know we were being watched, and fag in mouth with his back to us all was pissing up a wall. "Plong, Plong," we shouted. He turned. Fag still in mouth, zipping up his flies.

"I'll see you all in room 42 in 30 minutes", said Harbistone as he turned and walked off towards the main school building.

We were screwed and knew it. Rosie, Richard and me each got four strokes. Plong collected six, the maximum for any offence. Harbistone was a chunky, ex-rugby playing type of great physical strength, and he knew how to wield the axe, or cane in our case. Poor old Plong. Two extra just for a piss.

My dad got to know about this caning and asked me to show him the damage. The skin was red raw, and in long, large welts.

"I'm going to that school, and I'm going to see the headmaster", he said.

"Good, somebody needs to", I answered.

Now my dad was a trade union official, and in 1969 was to become a Councillor. He could argue the face off a gingerbread man.

Two days later at home he asked, "How long has that headmaster been at King Edwards?"

"About two years," I answered.

"I met him. Low enough to crawl under a snake with a top hat on, that one."

"Did you tell him about me?" I asked anxiously.

"Not just you, but about every caning that happens there. I told him that it would all be totally outlawed within a few years, so he might as well break that stick now and set an example to all the other school bullies."

"What did he say about that?"

"He grinned at me and shook his head. I wanted to shake his scrawny neck."

Remaining undaunted, we set out to cause more trouble. It was a strange time. We weren't nasty kids in any way. The world was changing. The school we attended was entrenched in the Victorian era still, and made little or no effort to escape from it. As the world changed it seemed that we wanted to go with it and release the shackles that held us all back. The only way we could do it was by rebellion. Our own form of rebellion.

We abused the teachers, the prefects, and stood up to them both verbally and physically. In a physics lesson once (I was crap at physics), we sat around tables of six or so, each seated on high stools. I was rude to the teacher, Mr. Mann, and he came for me with his hand formed in to a fist. I jumped from the stool, and raised it above my head. I swear to this day, if he had thrown a punch, I would have felled him with the stool. Fortunately, he saw the danger and backed off. I never heard any more of that incident.

In a chemistry lesson, again seated around long tables, me, Plong and Rosie took revenge on someone, a fellow pupil who had grassed on us. Before the beginning of the lesson, and still waiting for the teacher to enter the room, we put this lad to the floor, and kept him pinned there with our feet. He kept receiving just a few toe ends to the body as he squirmed to break free. He must have been hurting. The teacher entered the room and immediately asked where his star pupil was.

"No idea sir, not seen him", answered Plong

"Most unusual," remarked Mr. Littlewood.

Just then our victim squirmed very strongly and managed to get to his knees. "I'm here sir."

"What the devil are you doing down there boy?"

"I was, I was dizzy and tired sir."

"You should go to bed earlier at night instead of watching dreadful mumbo jumbo on television."

"Yes sir, I will sir in future. I promise."

To our victim's credit he had every opportunity to grass us, but never did. That incident could have had severe consequences for us.

We just carried on causing mayhem however. At that time on television The Untouchables starring Robert Stack as Elliot Ness, and Neville Bond as Al Capone was being shown. An American series made in the fifties it portrayed the gangster era of Chicago with Capone and his mob

Our little gang of four loved it.

We even had a protection racket running for a while taking money and cigarettes from innocent fellow pupils. The thoughts of it now makes me cringe and feel ashamed of myself. However, I always loved The Untouchables and proclaimed it as my favourite television show ever. That is of course until Peaky Blinders hit our screens in recent times. That series is different class.

During the six weeks summer holiday of 1967 I vowed to turn myself around, get my head down, and work harder. Starting in September I would be in a different class to Plong and Rosie. I would be in class 5G with Richard M. and Tony. S, both old mates of mine, and just like me at last chance saloon.

Apart from the bad behaviour and the trouble that followed, I should really have grasped 1967 and made more of it. My resentment for King Edward VII had left me with a strong feeling of revenge and bitterness.

I had many things in my favour, and didn't realise it. I had a fantastic family who supported me despite my failings. I had Christine who, as young as I was, I loved dearly.

I also had the films, the music, and just how good was the music that year?

My favourite band, The Doors, burst on to the scene with their debut album named after themselves (self-titled). Great tracks such as 'Light My Fire'; 'The End' and 'Break On Through'. The album in itself was as a soundtrack for a generation.

On June 1st 'Sergeant Pepper's Lonely Heart Club Band' was released. Although I bought it and played it constantly, I never really liked it too much. I just played it because everybody else did. How stupid!

Then the Monterey pop festival in California. I would have loved to have been there to see Jefferson Airplane, The Who, Grateful Dead, Hendrix, The Animals, Otis Redding, Mamas & Papas. Hendrix released the iconic album 'Axis Bold As Love' in December that year.

I didn't learn anything from being a prick. All I did was push myself on to the next phase of life, and that was to be the year 1968.

Chapter Ten
School's Out (1968)

All through 1968 I was continuing to deliver newspapers around Stannington estate. 100 Sheffield Star papers each night in all kinds of weather. Splitting the estate in to three, I delivered Roscoe area, Liberty, and all of Fairbarn.

I loved it, every minute of it. I got bitten by dogs, verbally abused by cheeky young kids, whistled at by 14-year-old girls, and soaked to the skin more often than not in those wild, windy hills of north-west Sheffield.

One of the great advantages of the job was that I got to see all the news first. All the sports news, the births, the marriages, the deaths, and of course the breaking news worldwide. I took in so much information that I often got very confused.

I got back home to 12 Liberty Hill one sunny evening in June 1968 after delivering the papers. My mother was in the kitchen, as usual. Breathlessly I shouted out "Do you know that Robert Kennedy is attending the jumble sale on Saturday at St. Marks Church Hall, Malin Bridge?"

"No, he's not love. He's dead. I've just seen his photo in The Star. He's been shot. He's dead. He won't be there Jack."

"What about the jumble sale? Will that go ahead?"

"Sit down Jack. You're overheated."

I sat down and thought about it. Suddenly I felt dizzy and that was it. I flaked out.

The next thing I remember was coming to with a cold, wet flannel on my wrist, and another on my forehead. Come to think of it, I had a similar occurrence over Easter that year. It was exceptionally warm for the time of year, and I had been kicking a ball about for a couple of hours with some other lads. What followed was the worst headache I have ever experienced, and two days in bed.

Some months later I had a spate of vomiting. Every time I got on a bus I just threw up. No warning, or nausea or gurgling stomach. I just kept puking.

On one occasion a woman sitting across from me on the bus put her hand on my shoulder and said "don't worry love, I've got a son who does that as well."

That left me thinking that I could possibly be at the front of a new protest movement against bus transport, instead of just me heaving away to my heart's content. There was now a growing army of pasty faced teenagers embarking upon a mission to decorate public service vehicles with a diverse display of stomach rejection.

My dad got so detective like about these events. Drugs were big news at the time. LSD, purple hearts, uppers, downers, marijuana, mushrooms. He had convinced himself that because I kept throwing up, I was definitely on something illicit. He searched all my books, bags, clothing, shoes and found nothing. I'm not surprised. I wasn't interested at all. Never had been. I found it hard to convince him. So, if ever I felt sick or dizzy, I just tried to pretend all was well even if I wanted to projectile vomit across the living room.

Maybe I did try drugs once in 1968. I'm not sure. After a GCE "O" level exam at school, we were given the rest of the day off. Steven E. and myself caught the bus back to Hillsborough, and walked up the hill to his house on May Road. He made us both beans on toast, we each had a cigarette, and then he hit me with, "Have you tried banana skins?"

"Why would I eat banana skins?" I asked.

"No you don't eat 'em. You bake 'em until they are black, then scrape off the ash and roll 'em in to cigarette papers."

"Sounds horrible," I answered.

"I'm going to do it anyway." said Steve.

He did, and it was vile. He scraped away the ash from two blackened banana skins, and rolled it in Rizla paper. Despite my protests I took a couple of drags. Suddenly that old familiar wave of nausea overcame me and I threw up a pile of bread and beans, on his mother's fireside rug.

"Watson, you idiot," he screamed. I couldn't even answer as my throat was full of beans.

"My mother's gonna kill me Watson. Help me get it cleaned up."

I shook my head vigorously, picked up my schoolbag, and ran for the outside.

"Come back here Watson, yer bastard."

I just kept on running, stopping every 50 yards or so to evacuate the beans on toast from my body. I reached the bus stop for my trip to Stannington, boarded the bus, and for once not throwing up on public transport, found my way home.

There was a lot going on that year. It was a very surreal time.

One night around 10.30pm after I had made sure Christine was safely on the bus to head home, I waited at Malin Bridge bus stop for the number 88 to take me home to Liberty Hill. I was alone at the stop, and there was no one anywhere else in sight. It was somewhat foggy, and behind me the rippling waters of the river Rivelin was all I could hear. I glanced at my watch. Just as I did so a voice beside me asked, "What time is it love?"

"Half past ten," I answered.

Next to me stood a small, frail woman of about 75 years of age. She wore a long gray coat, and a soft hat with a pin in it. She smiled and thanked me. I looked away to my left up the road. Nothing about. No cars, no buses, no people. I turned my head in an effort to make brief conversation with the woman. She had gone. In a matter of seconds the woman had completely disappeared. I looked over the wall in to the river. I strained my eyes to the right, to the left, and all around me. She was nowhere to be seen. A woman so small and aged could never have run the 75 yards to disappear on to Holme Lane in just six or seven seconds.

I put this down to an apparition. I still remember her appearance in detail. Maybe she was, and still is my guardian angel. If so, I owe her many favours. No banana skins were present at all during this happening.

If 1967 was the time of love, then 1968 was the time of hate. In Spring Martin Luther King was planning a national occupation of Washington DC, as a protest to be called the Poor People's campaign. However, on 4th April he was assassinated in Memphis, Tennesee by James Earl Ray. His death was followed by spontaneous riots across the United States.

Over the course of seven nights at least 43 people were killed, 2,500 injured, and 15,000 arrested. The vast majority of the rioters were black, angry and frustrated at the death of King. Of course all this bad news was miles away. The people of Great Britain trudged on in their workaday lives. Something they had been used to of course for a succession of generations. If you saw such things as the death of Mr. King on the news it shocked but didn't alter the daily lives of the British. The mind-set was that we had bigger fish to fry because we needed to shorten the working week and go on strike for one shilling extra per hour. These were the day to day affairs of importance at the time in our green and pleasant land.

Then we heard this in a speech in Birmingham. "As I look ahead, I am filled with foreboding. Like the Roman, I seem to see the River Tiber foaming with much blood."

Enoch Powell of course. This speech delivered in 1968 stopped all of us in our tracks. Suddenly, did we have a racially divided country just like the USA? There was much debate on the matter. We even spent a full hour debating the issue in economics at school.

A couple of days after the speech, me and Tony S were walking from school and in to town to catch the 88 bus home. Part of that journey took us through the Broomhall area. The area itself had had a recent influx of West Indian families, but there was no trouble at all. As we rounded a corner, painted on a wall in large white letters read the words POWELL IS A BASTARD. It raised a chuckle from us as we moved quickly along. The next day we did the same walk to town again. There on that very same wall it now read POWELL IS A STAR. Someone had made the effort to paint out the letters B, A, and D. Even greater chuckles ensued.

That was fantastic graffiti in graffiti's infancy, but not anywhere near the best I have seen. Many years later whilst travelling through Brixton, South London, a wall read FREE WINSTON SILCOTT. Directly underneath it in another style someone had scrawled WITH EVERY BOX OF CORNFLAKES.

The Vietnam war dragged on and on. There were large scale student riots in Paris. The Rolling Stones sang about "Street Fighting Man". It was their call to arms and it coincided with the Grosvenor Square riots in London. In Berlin, Mexico City, and Brazil protestors challenged the establishment.

Sometimes I look back and think this was probably our generation's finest hour. The Western World was at war with itself. Not just politically, but down on the streets. Many hippies had become yippies intent on protest, disquiet, and moderate revolution. We really had lost that loving feeling.

Then the big news of 1968 broke. Robert Kennedy had been assassinated. Shortly after midnight on 5th June in the kitchen of the Ambassador Hotel in Los Angeles, a Palestinian/Jordanian immigrant named Sirhan Sirhan stepped forward from the shadows and repeatedly fired a .22 calibre revolver at the Democratic presidential candidate. Kennedy had been hit three times. The fatal shot entered behind the right ear. He died 26 hours later in the Good Samaritan Hospital despite extensive neurosurgery.

This killing hurt me, and hurt me more at the time than the killing of John F. Kennedy. Okay, I was five years older, more worldly, yet also more aware of the trauma and troubles of the decade we were living through. Bobby Kennedy represented a new dawn for the world, and I and many others believed that he would achieve this. A cloud, as dark as can be, hung over the world when he passed. As someone said at the time "We shall NOT overcome."

Bobby Kennedy said many times, and this was quoted by his brother on the day of his farewell, "Some men see things as they are and say why? I dream things that never were and say why not?"

During that same month of June, and my last few weeks at King Edward VII Grammar School, I was studying to take more GCE "O" level examinations. I had smartened up my act, and was really making an effort to pick up a few more passes to add to the three I already had. I had every intention to leave school at the end of July. Not too may King Edward pupils ever left at the end of their fifth year as they mostly went on to take "A" levels and then aim for a university place.

The exams we sat both at "O" level and "A" level were set by the Oxford and Cambridge schools examination board. They were generally more "testing" it was rumoured. Whatever they were, I had no intention to take my education further. I wanted to get out of that hellhole and make some money, or at least be free from the constraints that dreadful establishment placed upon me.

So, during that month I took a further five exams, and got three passes, giving me a total of six passes in all. I was relatively quite pleased with that.

After one exam (I can't remember which), I left school about 12.30pm, and headed to meet Christine. She was due for her half hour break from work at 1pm, and I hadn't seen her for days. I turned up outside her place of work just as she was coming out of her employer's door, along with her workmates. She waved to me, and one of her colleagues burst out laughing.

"Is that your boyfriend?", another one asked. Christine smiled and nodded politely. Suddenly there were five or six girls all laughing and pointing at me. Then I caught on. I was wearing school uniform. Christine walked over to me smiling and gave me a big kiss, full on.

"I'm going to take some stick for this", she said, pointing at my clothing.

"Forget it," I replied, "tarts anyway".

"Jack, no they're not," came her startled response.

Anyway, she then bought me a sandwich, and to this day one of the best I have ever had. Fried luncheon meat and fried onions on a bread cake (for the uninitiated, a bap, cob, roll etc, depending on where in the country you were brought up).

One month later with my trusty transistor radio playing "Hurdy Gurdy Man" by Donovan, I walked out of the school that had been my captor for five years. I handed my leaving report to my dad and he shook his head. If it was bad, I didn't care anyway. He passed me the report. In almost all subjects

I had performed well. The comment from the headmaster implored me to change my mind, and go on back to school in September. He suggested that I could get good "A": level results and proceed further to obtain a degree in English or History.

I couldn't forget the way they had been with me when I refused to give up the girl I loved. There was no way I would change my mind, and I hoped the headmaster and his bunch of sadistic colleagues would fall off the end of the Earth.

The music of 1968 was almost a backdrop to the mayhem and anarchy that was the year. "Fire" by The Crazy World Of Arthur Brown; "Wheels On Fire" by Julie Driscoll and The Brian Augur Trinity.; The album "Wheels of Fire", by Cream. The flowers of 1967 had turned to the fire and revolt of 1968.

"Jumping Jack Flash" by the Stones, and the excellent version of "With A Little Help From My Friends", by the incredible Sheffielder, Joe Cocker, were real highlights.

Of course all these great recordings were tempered in the pop charts at the time by successes from Des O'Connor, Leapy Lee, Richard Harris and Malcolm Roberts. It wasn't just teenagers who bought records.

On the movie scene we had to endure Space Oddysey. What was that about? Bullitt starring Steve McQueen at his coolest represented just about the best film released that year. Then of course starring the gorgeous Jane Fonda we watched Barbarella, the film in which Jane, oozing sexuality, is placed inside the Orgasmatron as Duran Duran played by Milo O'Shea presses the vital keys.

On 31st August, 1968, I witnessed the finest game of football one ever could see. In front of 51,900 spectators Manchester United, the new champions of Europe, and with a team containing great names such as Law, Best, Charlton, were leading Sheffield Wednesday 4-2 at half time. The second half was a complete turn round as the Owls stormed out of the blocks and finished up at the final whistle winning 5-4. A fantastic memory.

In late December 1968, Ethel Kennedy, wife of the murdered Robert, gave birth to their eleventh child, Rory. It was a very fitting, iconic end to this most apocalyptic year. Well done to the Kennedys for having the final word yet again.

Chapter Eleven
Marching, Charging Feet, Boy

My intention when starting this work was in some way to keep it all light and humourous. Unfortunately, the next few pages are pretty dark. Sorry.

From the age of five my dad had taught me basic self-defence moves. How to jab and then cross, hook, uppercut etc. At the age of eight I had a pair of boxing gloves bought me for Christmas. The tuition continued.

If someone grabs you from behind in a neck hold, use instant elbow on your opponent's gut. If that fails employ a back heel to the shin. If you are attacked with a knife, stand sideways on and use one arm to parry (before running away).

I was certainly no expert, but I knew the basics, and it served me well.

During the early sixties wrestling was televised twice a week. The venues were such places as Bolton Town Hall and Sheffield Somme barracks. The protagonists were people such as Jackie Pallo, Mick McManus, Bert Royal, Billy Two Rivers, and countless other fanciful names. Fighting was popular, no doubt about it. Wrestling provided great viewing, and by watching and studying you could learn and perfect many moves. The Boston Crab was way out of my league though. I wasn't strong enough to hold down a sandwich never mind a struggling human body aged five or over.

My dad used to watch all boxing shown on television. Mostly it was amateur boxing, for instance Great Britain versus USA. In 1961, the British team beat the USA by ten bouts to nil. I watched with my dad, and he was really excited by the action and the score line. Billy Walker and Alan Rudkin were in the British team, and they both went on to have very successful professional careers.

In those days, the names I knew of, and watched and listened for were Brian London, Henry Cooper, Frankie Taylor, Sonny Liston, Floyd Paterson. That is until Cassius Clay came along and changed the whole face of the sport forever.

That was my background in the pugilistic arts. In a way it simply soaked in to me. Because we had fought in two world wars in the space of thirty odd years, male aggression and bravado became almost inbuilt. Stories would abound of bravery and heroism in everything you listened to, watched and read well in to the fifties and sixties. It was almost part of our DNA. How did we match up to it with no war to fight? Simple. We waged war on each other.

It was a dark winter night in 1967 on Middlewood Road, Hillsborough. 15 years old, we were just staring blankly in to a toy shop window. There were six of us. Me, Christine, Rosie, Janet, Steve E, and Tony S. Two cars drew up across the road from us. "Run its Carrelli," Tony shouted. The rest of us didn't have a clue what he was on about, but we ran anyway. There were six or seven of them aged about 19, and all wearing suits.

I was the first to suffer. Punched on the jaw, I went backwards through a shop window. The girls ran and hid, Tony and Steve scattered. Rosie got the worst of it. As he ran away one of the gang grabbed his paisley scarf from him. Stupidly he stopped to retrieve it. He was punched and kicked for a full minute.

The gang climbed back in to their cars and drove off shouting, screaming and laughing. Extracting myself from the shards of glass that lay around me, I ran down the road to find Rosie slumped in a shop doorway bleeding around the face and holding his ribs. The girls came by and despite us asking passers-by for help, nobody wanted to know.

Rosie had a broken nose and ribs, and a couple of teeth missing. He was never allowed to come out with us again. We later heard that on the previous night the same gang had struck at Hillsborough Corner, and had held down a couple of lads and slit their eyelids with razors. I believe the gang were from Parson Cross area, and we only ever knew the one name.

Listen to John Cooper Clarke and his "Kung Fu International". It's very reminiscent of that night.

In those days, just about everybody was up for a fight, especially at school.

In Malin Bridge schoolyard I witnessed a gruesome contest between a pair of 11 year olds. I was nine at the time. The two combatants, who I knew very well, went at the fight hammer and tongs. One of these lads, when in his teens, had gathered such a fearsome reputation that everyone treated him with unnecessary respect.

On this day, the two of them began to trade punches until the "lesser" one was being well beaten, but refused to give up. As the fearsome one went to throw a punch to finish him, lesser thrust a penknife in to fearsome's thigh. The blade and handle protruded from the inside of fearsome's thigh.

74

Everybody took a pace backwards. We'd never seen junior school scrapping on this level. Fearsome looked down at the knife, then grabbed the handle and pulled the blade out, dropping it to the floor (not exactly text book actions, but he was angry). He then waded in to lesser and gave him a real hammering. It took three teachers to pull fearsome away snarling, cursing, spitting. I have labelled these two lads fearsome and lesser because it just would not be fair to even give a hint to their names after all these years. Besides, they might come and get me.

A year or so later, in the same spot in the schoolyard, after a few words, a lad, Paul.K, threw a punch and caught me over the eye. I jabbed him, then caught him with a good right cross. He came back with "one over the top". I ducked, and his fist smashed in to the stone wall I had my back against. He screamed as his knuckles poured blood, and his fingers became misshapen. If that punch had landed on me, I would have gone down. He was beefy.

At King Edward VII the scent of aggro was in the air constantly. You only had to look at somebody wrongly .and you were threatened. One day in the fourth year, so 1966-67, Rosie, Plong and me were walking along an empty corridor. Around the corner came a lad I think was named Gatling. He was in the year below us but was tall, stocky, and probably useful. He tried to walk through the three of us. I shouldered him and walked on. The next thing I knew was him hung around my neck, trying to drag me to the floor. My elbow shot in to his gut, and he fell away, doubled up. He straightened up, and backed against a wall. I hit him a dozen times in the gut with rapid punches, left and right, and he slid back down the wall. I let him get up and he held out his hand to shake on it. "No chance tosser and don't ever mess with us again." Not clever Jack.

Sometimes at King Edward, if pupils were caught fighting the teachers would invite the two to meet in the gym at 4pm. There a gym mat would be laid out, and a bucket of water would be placed at opposite corners. The pair would then be told to strip, put on shorts and nothing else. Each lad would have his own second, and you were to box for three times three minute rounds. Win by knockout or surrender. No points decision. Boxing gloves were provided from the gym's stock cupboard. The referee was a teacher. Some contests were far too one-sided, and yet some kids who were getting leathered would never pack in. Blood was everywhere. I never got to fight in one of those contests thankfully. The blood splattered mats would be used again next day for PE.

Everyone was scrapping everywhere. Love and peace in the sixties? That's just a marketing image for people trying to sell overplayed number ones from the music of that era.

Then of course there was the mods and rockers. At opposite ends of the youth explosion, these two groups dressed differently, spoke differently, rode different vehicles, and literally hated each other. The rockers were generally older, and still were in love with the 1950s' rock'n'roll of Bo Diddly, Gene Vincent, Eddie Cochran. They wore leather, chewed gum, and rode motorcycles.

The mods appeared cleaner, neater, wore suits and parkas, rode scooters, and listened to the Who, Small Faces, and American soul.

The brawls between the two groups in the mid-sixties, particularly 1964, became stuff of legend. Margate, Bournemouth, and Clacton bore the brunt of Bank Holiday violence. Often, with deckchairs as weapons, police found it hard to control the wild, unruly mob behaviour. At Brighton over Whitsun weekend the fighting lasted two days and moved all along the coast to Hastings and back. Watch Quadrophenia for the battle of Brighton. The violence eventually spread northwards, and one night in 1966 at Sheffield speedway as me and my cousin John took a walk around the back of the stand, some older rocker types approached us.

"What are you doing around here son?"

"Nothing," I replied, "Just walking."

He smashed an empty Guinness bottle on a wall, and pushed it to within an inch of my face.

"You're young mods, aren't you?"

"No we're not," I answered nervously.

"What's with the hipsters and chukka boots then?"

"My mother bought 'em for me"

The bottle came nearer my face.

"Look" said the rocker, "just piss off and don't let me see you here again."

We duly pissed off, and didn't return to the speedway for a few weeks.

From 1964-65, this violence amongst the youth began to manifest itself at football matches. Journalists often write about the 1980s being the worst decade for trouble at football. Well, no it wasn't. It was in fact at its worst in the seventies when 500 per side would take to the streets. Or in Man Utd's case it was probably more like 5,000. However, it all began in the sixties.

In October 1966, the Owls played Fulham at Hillsborough, and drew 1-1. As five or six of us walked along Penistone Road, a handful of Fulham fans dressed in Clockwork Orange gear (years before the film was released) came up behind us. One grabbed my parka hood and dragged me to the ground. They all started kicking me. Suddenly the one who had started it all fell to the ground beside me, his skull pissing out blood. I jumped up quickly, and we all got out of the way. It transpires that my cousin Peter B had seen the kicking I was getting and launched a lump of steel at the Fulham fans from about 10 yards. Good shot.

A few weeks later we played Stoke City at Hillsborough. Stoke fans were on our kop throwing all sorts of missiles. Bottles and bricks flew everywhere. Then came a barrage of fireworks. Bangers to be precise. I smelled burning. I realised a banger had lodged between my shirt collar and my neck. I pulled at my collar and the firework hit the ground and exploded. One second later and I would have forever been seriously scarred. (My guardian angel at play again?) With twenty minutes of the game remaining, and losing 3-1, Peter B and me made our exit. We marched straight down to the away fans car park. We launched a bombardment of missiles at parked coaches, making a mess, and then made our way to places nearer home. I was still pondering what could have become of my face that afternoon.

In December that year I travelled with my cousin John to watch us play at Nottingham Forest. The match passed peacefully, and ended 1-1. As we began to walk out over Trent Bridge after the game I reminded John that the Forest fans had a reputation for throwing opposition fans in to the river from the bridge. No sooner had I mentioned it than we heard them from behind us.

"Sha la la la Hennessey, who the fuckin hell is he? The greatest player in history", they sang.

I looked over my shoulder and there must have been a dozen of them. All older than us, and all long-haired types.

"Turn and face them John," I said.

"What are you mad," he answered.

"No, just do it."

He did. So, there we stood. A couple of skinny 15 year olds facing up to a dozen long haired lads of 17 baying for our blood, and with one of England's largest rivers inconveniently flowing along either side of us. I reached in to my pockets, and brought out on each hand a set of old fashioned brass school compasses, fully extended.

"Right, first one near me gets this down his throat." Silence reigned.

"John, just keep backing off slowly."

A couple of Forest edged forward. I thrust the compasses outwards. They edged backwards. 20 seconds silence ensued.

"Run John, run."

We turned and ran all the way to the coach park about 300 yards away. Some of the Forest fans kept up the chase, some didn't bother. We had enough in our legs to get away.

Over the next couple of years, we had run ins with Leeds, Man City, Chelsea, Newcastle, and of course our old friends from Bramall Lane, Sheffield United. Sadly, at one game at Bramall Lane both sets of fans were guilty of throwing acid in bottles at each other. Many people were burned on their hands and faces that night. That's not cricket, no matter who you support.

Finally, one last word for my school pal, Tony S. who despite being a rocker and a Blade always stood by me when things got "messy" on the streets.

Chapter Twelve
It Was A Teenage Wedding (1969)

"This is one small step for a man, one great leap for mankind."
"Frankly Neil, I don't give a damn". Is that another quote?
I really didn't give a damn. I must have been on 20th July, 1969, the most disinterested person on the planet with regards to the Moon landing.

Christine was pregnant and I was a very worried young man. In fact she was a very worried young woman. Earlier that month she had paid her first visit to her doctor to see what had caused her to stop seeing a period since March, and had also caused her to be sick and make her belly swell. We knew it wasn't a gastric problem. We knew she was well and truly pregnant.

Her mother accompanied her to the doctor's surgery. I sat outside her house on the front step awaiting their return. Christine's dad sat with me. He smoked a Park Drive, and I smoked a Player's No.6. We didn't speak.

Christine and her mother returned. Her mum's face was like thunder. Her dad remained silent. We all went in to the house.

"Right" said her mum. "You'd better decide what you're going to do. You've made your bed, so you can bleedin' lie on it." She had a way with words.

So, over the course of the next few weeks we had to decide just what we were going to do with our future, and our baby's future. We were both 17, and in those days, despite the progress that had been made in all walks of life, the pregnancy of a young single woman was still frowned upon. We decided to make a decision on our future by 1st August.

I had been working since November 1968. Having left school in July I decided to just relax for a few months, and look for a job in a leisurely fashion.

The first interview I had was with the Zurich Insurance Company and I was offered the position of junior clerk on a starting weekly wage of £8 per week. I didn't accept the offer. For some strange, unthinkable reason I had my heart set on working for Sheffield City Council in a role within the housing department or something similar. Another life changing decision perhaps on my part. Look at the size of Zurich Insurance now with their swish head office on the outskirts of Cheltenham. Who's to know? I seem to remember people saying stuff like "get a job with the council in the town hall, and you'll never be short of a job." How times have changed! I couldn't even get an interview. My focus had to turn elsewhere.

I saw a job advertised in the Sheffield Star and rang the number from a public call box. It was a job in industry. Something that I hadn't considered, and wasn't prepared for. It was November though. I had left school some 14 weeks earlier and I was getting fed up of playing Subbuteo day in, day out. I was probably the oldest paperboy in Sheffield and people stared at me when I delivered to them because I was needing a shave.

The company interviewing me was Brown & Tawse Tubes Ltd of Darnall, Sheffield. So, I travelled on two buses to the interview. The first from Stannington to town, and then another bus to Darnall travelling through the grimy east end of the city. It was like another world. Having spent the previous three years on the clean, fresh hills of north west Sheffield, I now found myself transported in to the heartland of our famous industrial city.

The interview with Mr. D.K.Rae went well, and we seemed to have a certain understanding. Mr. Rae was probably mid-thirties, and spoke in that soft, Scottish educated tone that at the same time is both endearing yet commanding. He was, I believe, a descendant of one of the families that had started the company around 100 years previously.

I was offered the job of trainee sales clerk, and was advised that I would be paid the princely sum of seven pounds, 10 shillings per week. I accepted instantly. So, once more another snap decision that would shape the rest of my life.

At the end of November, I started work there, and despite the travelling, I really did enjoy this new phase of my life. The people were friendly, and helped me whenever they could. Brown& Tawse in Sheffield, in a new building were stockists of steel pipes and fittings, and also had a stainless steel department attached. Across the road from our offices was the fabrication plant. The girls at Brown & Tawse were very nice as well I might add.

All this of course was totally alien from the day to day academic background I had been immersed in for the previous five years. I hadn't missed school at all, and I quickly tried to forget the pain and drudgery it had inflicted on me. Brown& Tawse didn't cane me. They didn't give me homework or detention. They allowed me to smoke, in fact positively encouraged it.

I felt uncomfortable about 1969. It didn't grasp me like the previous three or four years had done. Maybe I was maturing, or maybe I had a sense of the future. Who knows? It just seemed a dark sort of depressing year. We didn't get to the cinema as much that year. The films released were by and large unappealing. I remember watching Where Eagles Dare at the ABC. That, as I recall, was on a wide screen as we were seated just a few rows from the front, a bit overpowering. Anyway, it was an okay. film, and of course Christine kept nudging me and smiling every time Clint Eastwood appeared. My response was simply "I'm better looking than him." I still think I am. Mind you he is about 85 now.

Easily the best two films of that year were Midnight Cowboy, and Easy Rider. Great movies starring great actors in Jon Voight, Dustin Hofmann, Dennis Hopper, and Jack Nicholson. You could feel through both storylines that they were almost attempting to edge their way out of the frivolous, flippant, movie making of the last couple of years, and move towards the challenging bigger, bolder world of the seventies. Both great films with great storylines.

Well before 1st August, Christine and I had made our minds up on the future. We had two alternatives only. We could get married and bring up our baby as any married couple would. The problem was that we had little money, and had no real prospects of getting any in the near future. I was still working hard earning my £7 ,10 shillings a week, and Christine in her job was being paid something similar, but she of course would need to finish work because of her pregnancy before long.

Our other alternative was for us to remain single, and to continue to live each with our parents. I would support financially as best I could, and Christine would bring up our baby with the help of her family.

We made the choice to get married. The hospital had given Christine a date around Christmas for the birth, and we were now at the end of July. So plans were drawn up for us to marry on 20th September at Owlerton St. John's Church. Christine's mother said we could live with them until we found somewhere suitable.

God Almighty, it really was a tough period for us. I would be 18 on the day before the wedding, and Christine would be 18 in December. We had but a few pounds in our pockets, and we were worried sick for our future. As people kept pointing out, we weren't the first, and we wouldn't be the last. There was as mentioned a certain stigma attached to our situation even in the so called liberated days of 1969.

As I walked past Mr. Rae's office door at Brown & Tawse he called me. "Jack, come on in. Close the door behind you."

"Oh no," I thought, "he's only going to sack me. What will I do then?"

Mr. Rae looked at me closely for a moment, then with a strange sort of half smile said, "I hear that you are about to get married, and you have a baby on the way."

"Yes, that's right, we're getting married in September." I replied.

"OK, then let me try and help you. I want you to take on the new position of purchasing officer. This will be a job where you will constantly be reviewing all our stocks, and you will be responsible for placing purchase orders on our suppliers. The job will be one of responsibility as we need to monitor our stock levels to keep and grow our existing customer base. I believe you can do this job Jack. I've been watching your progress."

"Oh thank you," I modestly replied.

"So, Jack because of this, I will if you accept this job, be increasing your pay to £12 per week."

"Yes, I accept. I'll do it. I can do that." I spluttered in reply.

"I'll give you all the training you need, and best of luck with it, but heaven knows how you will survive on £12 per week."

"Thank you, Mr. Rae, we'll do our best."

I left the room almost bowing as a departing servant might do. The man had given me a fighting chance.

On 20th September 1969, our wedding day came along all too soon. I climbed out of bed and looked out of the bedroom window from 12 Liberty Hill. It looked to be a bright sunny day. I felt shocking. Stupidly, the night before I had been out and arrived home in a dreadful, drunken state. As a double celebration for my 18th birthday and as a stag do, I had been persuaded to meet up with a few people in the Charles Turnbull pub on Liberty Hill. From there we visited a further five pubs in Stannington. At that time Stannington above the Sportsman pub was classified as being in the old district of Yorkshire West Riding, and did not belong at all in Sheffield.

In the Hare & Hounds we had become a bit raucous, and the West Riding police had followed us around in to the Crown & Glove, and the Rose & Crown. They walked us down to the Sheffield boundary stone across from the Sportsman and left us, warning us not to come back. They just didn't like us townies at all.

I vomited myself to sleep forgetting that I was to be married the very next day.

"Jack, you look shocking," exclaimed my mother as I entered the living room.

"Do him some bacon and eggs, that should put a lining on his stomach," remarked my dad, looking up from his newspaper.

I immediately felt sick and shook my head to say no. I forced a cup of tea down in a few seconds to re-hydrate. It was almost as if I had an asbestos lined mouth. I sank another one immediately. I put my head in my hands and stared at the floor. The carpet was the reddest article I had ever seen. All my senses were exaggerated. I wanted to shut my eyes and just sleep for days.

"You don't have to do this Jack if you don't want, you know," said my father.

"Do what?", I answered weakly.

"Get married."

"Oh God," I thought. "Married, married. I am getting married."

It wasn't the thought of marriage that bothered me. It was the thought of the fuss and palaver that I was about to endure. I really didn't need it. Flowers, kisses, handshakes, confetti. At that moment any confetti landing on my head would have felt like half house bricks.

"Can I have some more tea?" I didn't know if I was whispering or shouting.

The marriage was to take place at 3.00pm at Owlerton church. At 2.00pm my best man, cousin John arrived, and at 2.20pm so did the cars to take us to Owlerton. Feeling a little better I had dressed quickly and kept slapping my own face in an attempt to put some colour in my cheeks. It didn't work. I still looked like Marley's ghost.

2.50pm and the church was filling. I talked with John. My mouth was like the bottom of a baby's pram (all shit and biscuits). My head pounded. The organ started to play "The Wedding March' and everyone in the church rose to their feet. I wasn't nervous. I felt myself smiling the sad smile of a half-wit clown.

Suddenly Christine was beside me. She looked beautiful. She held a bouquet close to her chest to cover the growing child inside her. At that moment she meant more to me than anyone or anything I had ever known before.

The reverend Christopher Whitehead commenced the ceremony, and as young as we were, or maybe as drunk as I was, we didn't mumble our lines or stumble over the procedure. We exchanged rings, and we were man and wife.

The reception was at the Castle Inn, Dykes Hall Road, Hillsborough, about half a mile from the church. Everyone duly arrived and we filled the room upstairs. I could smell the alcohol as I entered the pub, and a feeling of nausea kept sweeping over me.

Jack and Christine on their wedding day

A salad meal of ham and lettuce and tomatoes was enjoyed, and speeches were made. Toasts were given to all and sundry. My dad, a speech maker supreme remarked that "Jack and Christine are both still babbies, and they now have another one due soon." He called on everyone to rally round and help us as best they could.

With the routine procedures over the bar opened, and we played some records. No DJ of course. We couldn't afford one. So, a few of us took turns to play selected 45rpm discs. Everything was going well. The drinks were flowing, people were dancing, smiling and generally having a good time.

Then it happened. Some dick from the pub downstairs crept up in to our privately hired room and started dancing amongst the wedding guests. I watched him for a while, carefully checking on his movements, his mood and his conversation. Suddenly he grabbed my mother around the waist and pulled her close to him. At this point I'd had enough of watching him, and jumped to my feet.

"What are you doing up here?" I yelled.

"And who are you?" he replied.

"I'll show you who I am," I screamed as I leapt towards him. He raised his fist at this point and everybody jumped in to separate me from him.

"Jack, it's not worth it," I heard.

"Jack, we'll get rid of him," came another shout.

Then my dad appeared, and lifting the intruder by the throat, walked him to the top of the stairs, and cast him downwards.

I could hear the noise and arguments going on downstairs and began to look for Christine. She was sitting with her mother who accused all we Watsons of being thugs and bullies. The music had been switched off by now, and someone pushed some money in my hand and suggested me and Christine get a taxi back to her home on Herries Road. We took the advice and the money and left the Castle via the front door on Dykes Hall Road. Outside stood my grandad, my dad, and uncle Alan Bratton in a tight group, all with their jackets off, and sleeves rolled up. Coming up the road towards the Castle was another group shouting, "are you lot Watsons? We are O'Neills, and we're here to sort it out."

"Get in the taxi quick Jack. Get Christine out of here," my dad shouted. The taxi had just arrived.

I did just that even though I wanted to stay. Nobody ever told me what happened after we left, but I guess it just fizzled out, or the police turned up. I heard some time later that there had been a feud going back to the

1930s between the Watsons and the O'Neill's in the Rudyard Road area of Hillsborough.

What a 24 hours it had been. My introduction to adulthood had been very eventful.

On the 31st December 1969, we were in a very perilous place. Not just Christine, myself, and our unborn baby, but the whole world. The Cold War was still getting colder. The world's leaders were seemingly incapable and incompetent. We were staring in to a void. The prospects for the new decade that now faced us were terrifying. From the colourful optimism of the 1960s liberalism, we now on this last day of the decade were almost like rabbits caught in the headlights. We did not know what the world had in store for us.

Just after midnight my wife and I turned to each other, kissed and wished each other a happy New Year. She had a tear in her eye. I patted her pregnant belly and said "not long now love, just take things day to day."

We were doing just that for many years after.

Christine, aged 24, looking a little stressed as she pushes our Greg, 3, accompanied by Dawn, 6, in Skegness in 1976.

Epilogue

You often hear people quote the phrase "It's not where you are from, it's where you are going to that counts". Well, I understand that quote, but it certainly does not apply to me.

When people ask the question, "If you could go back to any age during your life, what age would you choose?" I always answer eight.

I cannot imagine anybody on Earth ever happier than I was when I was eight. I had the love and guidance of two fantastic parents. I had a full family of grandparents, aunts, uncles and cousins from both the Watsons and Bowers. I liked them all. They were all very good to me. Although I never liked school, I was always good at it.

In Malin Bridge junior and infant school I had the best school around. In the Hirsts, Swifts, Whomersleys and Bingleys I had great playmates on Proctor Place, and just up the road was my favourite football team who were only bettered by the famous Tottenham team of that time.

We had a brilliant cinema next door. We had a shop for every need within 20 yards walk. We had Hillsborough Park. We had everything in and around Proctor Place, except of course hot water, a bath, an indoor toilet and pest control. There's a compromise in everything. Naturally.

We had snow in winter, and sun in summer. None of your mixed-up seasons like now. In winter, you just needed some gloves, some wellies, and a sledge. In summer, just a pair of shorts and a handkerchief to wrap around your jubbly.

Life couldn't have been better, but nothing lasts. As puberty approached I began to see the world from different angles. Instead of bowling the perfect off break that pitches, turns sharply and nicks a bail enough to remove it, I dreamed of other things. Girls mostly. Nothing wrong with girls of course. Most wonderful, divine creatures. Until you get the wrong side of them.

Then came the music, and what a time to enjoy music. I loved the early beat/pop scene. It was a statement of revolution and defiance. I recall being 13 and staring through my overlong fringe walking to town on my way home from school singing to myself, "you really got me going, you got me so I don't know what I'm doing, oh yeah." The Kinks of course with that amazing beat and joyously simple lyrics. Perfection to represent our growing generation.

I could ask where is the novelty now in being 13? I don't know. I'm not knocking these misfits, not their fault. Somehow though the Xbox doesn't seem to drive adrenalin quite like a 30 yarder from Charlton, or a straight 6 from Sobers, or a guitar smashing minute from Hendrix. Whichever way I look at it, I feel blessed to have been born and raised in a slot in time where everything happened. No periods of tranquillity, but a period of relative peace. No periods of unity, but a period of forced change. No periods of divinity, but a period of spiritual growth.

GOD BLESS YOU ALL.